Maggie understands [illegible] ing. Psychopathy is b[illegible] inter- ested in feeling, and w[illegible]ories turn violent (as they frequently do), it's with a surreal emotional barbarity that distorts the entire world. You can mop up blood with any fabric. Maggie's concern is with the wound left behind, because the wound never leaves—it haunts. As a result, each of these stories leaves a wound of its own. Some weep, watching as you try (and fail) to recover. Others laugh. But never without feeling.

—B.R. Yeager, author of *Negative Space*

And once finished, I felt like my tongue had been misplaced, guts heavy and expanded ... gums numb with a tongue that'd been put elsewhere, my mouth clean around a pipe weaving up through pitch and shadow ... and well past ready, primed for delight, waiting but knowing I had already been filled to skin; crying shit, hearing piss, fingernails seeping bile, pores dribbling blood, soles slopping off and out to meet a drain mid-floor ... .

—Christopher Norris, author of *Hunchback '88*

Not to be so populist, but Siebert's work is both reminiscent and contrary to Ballard. Both of their works are about self-detonation, Ballard's were about sexual desire, while Siebert's are about its absence. But therein lies the rub: her most striking moments are those of connection, the sorts that transcend desire and passion, aromantic and extreme. Her stories illustrate one, larger truth: the only way to understand each other is to atomize ourselves.

—John Samuel Brown

Bonding is a handbook ... a map ... a guide ... full of laundry machines constructed out of plastic. Bonding transcends judgment ... read it ... absorb it like exhaust fumes ... soak it up like the smog in Cobble Hill soaks you up. This book is warmth ... the sort of temperature you find escalating from freeways ... off-ramps ... on-ramps ... bridges ... bitumen constructions. This book solves our problems ... with wet disintegration ... and apocalyptic preoccupations. Gift cards and button up shirts. Skin grafts in duffel bags ... license plates all Brooklyn-bound. This book is a travel guide to an unusual apartment ... full of skinny fingers stuck in a Styrofoam container ... full of buffalo chicken strips ... where everyone's almost naked anyway ... and if someone sneaks a blunt in under their armpit ... big deal. *Bonding* is steam on a conveyor belt ... mist inside your mouth. Pizza Hut and an obsession with the end of the world. My favourite things. Maggie Siebert once told us that death would not solve our problems ... one can only hope.

—Shane Jesse Christmass, author of *Belfie Hell*

Felt my ass tighten, release, tighten, release throughout my reading of Maggie's *Bonding*.

—Kyle Kirshbom

ɓonɗine

MAGGIE SIEBERT

BONDING

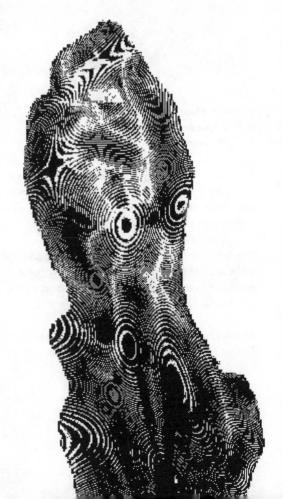

Parts of this book appeared, in somewhat different form, in *Hobart Pulp, Misery Tourism, Trash World, Witch Craft Mag, Surfaces*, and *SELFFUCK*.

Cover Design by Christopher Norris
Interior Design by Mike Corrao

ISBN: 978-1-954899-06-3

MAGGIE SIEBERT   BONDING

TABLE OF CONTENTS

"He was decapitated in an explosion of flame and glass fragments/Her body was found crushed into the dashboard/A mini-cam report described them as fine youngsters/They never got a chance to fulfill their career dreams"

— "Teen Love," No Trend

mes

He asks me if I understand what this place is and I say yes. We're standing in a room full of laundry machines and cleaning supplies. There's a large plastic table, upon which rests a stack of folded sheets and a styrofoam container full of buffalo chicken strips. He's been eating them since I arrived thirty minutes ago, grabbing one between his skinny fingers and slurping on it while he asks me questions.

"No," he says, sucking in another mouthful. The chicken strips aren't crispy anymore. Whole pieces of breading have slid off revealing soft white meat underneath. Their wetness disintegrates inside his mouth. "I mean do you under*stand* what this place *is?*"

The sign hanging ajar outside calls it Bodyworks Sauna. It's situated above a Quizno's and you have to walk up two flights of stairs. When you reach the top, a thick metal door with an electronic lock blocks your path. You buzz in only to be greeted by a second door. Behind a small piece of plexiglass, a guy checks your ID and asks if you'll be staying overnight or if you just need a locker. You pay twelve dollars and when you get inside, the sound of trashy eurohouse hits you like a wave. In the corners of your vision, men of all shapes and sizes mill around with towels wrapped around their waists, trying to get someone to make eye contact.

So yes, I say to him, I know what this place is.

"OK," he says, licking dabs of ranch off the corners of his mouth with his tongue. "Let me show you what you'll be doing."

We step out of this enclosed room and he leads me to a janitor's cart. There are a few bottles of Simple Green, some rags, a flashlight, a big trash can, and a garbage bag where I'm supposed to put dirty sheets.

He leads me to a room and bangs on the door. When he sees it's unoccupied, he pushes the door open and gestures me inside.

"As you can see, they're pretty small," he says, and yes, I can see that. A single twin mattress that takes up most of the room sits in one corner. A wastebasket in another. In this particular room, a glory hole connects to the room next door. It's cut into a piece of plywood on hinges, padlocked shut. I can't imagine sticking my dick in it.

He tells me when people are finished using the room and have turned their keys in for the night, we go in and turn the lights off. We shine the flashlight on the wall and around the floor to look for cum. When we do a pass this time, there's a huge half-dried load on the glory hole I didn't notice before. He sprays it with Simple Green and shows me how he wipes it with a rag.

Then he tells me to flip the mattress. We spray it with a bleach solution and flip it again and do the other side. I ask him if I need to wipe it around and he says no, not really, this isn't the Ritz-Carlton. He sprays the floor, then drops a rag and kicks it around with his foot. There's nothing in the wastebasket so he says we're good, we're done, and shuts off the light.

"That's really all there is to it," he says, and I nod.

For the rest of the day, he teaches me to use the register, how to wash sheets and distribute room keys and check lockers and make sure guys aren't bringing in anything too dangerous. No booze, no needles, no knives. And all night, different guys come and go, stripping down to towels and groping around the labyrinthine hallways. There's no way of telling how big it is from the outside, but it's much larger than I expected. There are nearly forty private rooms, and only a few of them are bigger than the one I saw. A few are even smaller. No outside light gets into the building, and the walls are painted black.

They prowl around these hallways and make eye contact and talk a little until they decide whether or not they want to go to a room together. Most of the doors are shut. I patrol the hallways with my cart and knock on doors and spray cum away. The *unts-unts-unts*es blare from hidden speakers, punctuated by moans and wet slaps. I hear someone getting his dick sucked, saying, "Fuck yeah, bro," to whoever is doing the job.

Of course, it's not all cruising and of course there are guys paying for it. But they're paying for it from older guys. Everybody is at least thirty, but the people with overnight rooms are all prostitutes in their fifties and sixties. One of them is a blind queen in a leotard. She's bald and wearing a big wig. She swipes her cane across the floor and slaps the walls and occasionally comes to the window and asks for a new towel or something, and I give it to her. She asks if she can go outside for a cigarette every half hour and comes back with a new guy, and I look him in the eyes and wish Hell upon him.

The night grows later and more people show up. The busier it gets, the less stringent we are about checking for contraband. Everyone's almost naked anyway, and if someone sneaks a blunt in under their armpit, big deal.

But the guy in the black hoodie stands out. He wouldn't strip down to a towel like everyone else. Nobody is paying him much interest. I peg him as insecure and don't say anything because my boss doesn't say anything. When he pays, he asks for a room for just a few hours and we tell him he'll need to wait for a little while before it's ready. He comes back and asks three more times before somebody finally vacates a room and I get to clean it.

I push my cart through the hallway to find the vacant room. The guy crosses my path at an intersection. It strikes me how this building is like a playset for a make-believe city. The flow of traffic congregates around certain gathering areas; saunas, the more attractive guys' rooms, the gym equipment that muscle freaks fuck on. I need him to get out of my way so I can get to his room and I tell him so.

He doesn't speak English very well, and once again asks me if his room is ready. His hood is up and he leers at me. His eyes glisten against the overhead light, bloodshot and huge, like he's afraid. I tell him one more time that I'm getting to it right now. He smiles.

"Okay," he says. "Yeah, sure. Okay."

I find his room and open the door. The sheets are already gone, and all that's in the trashcan is a cigarillo filter and a condom wrapper. I note to watch out for condoms in the laundry and start spraying everything down.

He appears in the doorway. I don't hear him—I feel his presence while I'm bent over wiping down a particularly stubborn load near where the wall meets the floor. He blocks the whole exit with his mass.

"Do you like your job?" he asks from the hallway.

"It's a job," I say. What I want to say is no, I don't, I don't know why I'm working here. I hate sex. if I could get away with it, I would stab or strangle or bludgeon every guy who's ever paid for it, and I'd start with the guys who have been fucking that blind girl. But I just scrub harder at the load and hope it'll be over soon.

I feel him inch closer, so I turn around. He hasn't crossed into the tiny room yet. His hoodie is still on, but he's pulled his cock out from behind the towel. He tugs at it and a thin spurt of sludge that looks green in the light oozes from the tip. His dick is cherry red and eclipsed by his fist. He looks at me and I look at him and I start laughing and he's smiling but not laughing. He keeps tugging, slowly.

"No," I say, "I'm working, get out of here."

He doesn't move. I stand up and grasp the doorknob with both hands and shove the open door toward him. He blocks it with his body and checks it out of my hands. I act on pure instinct and look around for something I can defend myself with.

He keeps jerking himself and holds the door open with his free hand, his towel around his ankles.

There is nobody in the hallway that will help me.

He lets go of his dick and kicks his towel out of the way. He raises his foot to take a step toward me. From there I imagine him forcing me onto the mattress and then I don't want to imagine anymore. I can only think of one thing to do, so I do it. I ball my hand into a fist and wind it back and sink it into his pudgy stomach with everything I have in me.

When I expect it to stop, it keeps going. His flesh suctions tight around my fist. I don't fully comprehend the feeling, so I just keep pushing. My force pushes him from the doorway into the adjoining wall outside the room. He slaps against the painted particle board, his head snapping forward then back like a whip crack. The wall is cracked and dust rains from the ceiling. My fist goes deeper until I feel the vertebrae of his spine brush against my knuckles and a bassy pop splits his stomach open. He hits the floor, my arm elbow deep inside of his guts, and I scream.

He's still laughing, trying to get a free hand back down to his prick. I try to wrench my hand from inside him but a great suction like a vacuum sealer pulls it deeper inside. I swipe around wildly, feeling for an orifice I might be able to widen but find nothing, just kidneys and his gallbladder and his distended stomach. It's a million degrees inside.

He's down on the floor now and I'm there with him. He's flailing for his cock. I scrape at any meat where my fingers can find purchase in the hope he'll have to spit me back out. He's spitting up blood, a sputtering I understand to be laughter. The whole hallway smells like blood and shit.

He looks me in the eyes like he loves me.

"Further," he says.

I try to pull my arm out again, but the suction is so tight around my elbow it feels like I'll break it, so I stop.

"Further in," he gurgles. Specks of bloody saliva dot my face and eyelids. I feel so much rage. I steady myself against the ground and force my arm deeper. My fist goes past his stomach and into his chest cavity. His wet ribs creak as I plow through them, a xylophonic dinging emanating from his open mouth.

He howls as I punch deeper, into his neck. Some of the pressure gives away, even though I'm nearly up to my shoulder. I can't get out of him yet, and I can't make the smell of his insides vacate my nose. All I can do is destroy a little more of him.

He can't talk over the swollen lump curled below his neck, and I don't want him to. I pull him to a sitting position and push higher, higher, higher until at last my fist bursts through, a wave of hot air hitting my fingers as they wiggle in his open mouth. I grasp his lower jaw like a ladder rung and slam him back into the wall over and over again, his top teeth gnashing at my knuckles.

He screams one last time before I hear a wet splat against the concrete floor and I realize he's finally come. He shudders hard and then goes limp. The orifice around my shoulder does too, and my arm slides out easily, along with everything that

was once contained inside him. His skin hangs limp and loose around his bones and fat deposits.

I gaze down at my hand. Bits of him are stuck under my fingernails.

Another mess to clean.

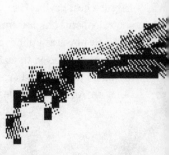

OPPORT

JRITIES

It was right outside the gas station that I hit the guy.

At least, I thought I did.

It's not my fault that my memory isn't the best. I did cage fighting for a while, and it's not a lie to say I had a few minor head injuries; concussions. I can still remember most things. The important stuff. Like, my birthday. I just had it. 10/17/92. See, that wasn't even a problem.

But sometimes things that just happen, especially things that happen kind of fast, are tough for me. It gets a little blurry.

And you know, how was I supposed to know this gas station would have a casino attached? A casino with drinks?

I'm driving to Seattle. I'm driving a piece of shit car, but it's reliable, in its own way. I'm feeling the open road. I'm getting highway hypnosis. A guy I used to fight with has a new job selling this nutrition powder. He told me I could come work under him, and I'd just been thinking about how I could use a job, so I figured this was some kind of sign. This was an opportunity worth exploring.

I've been driving for a long time, and it's just about sunset. I'm on the Interstate but I don't know where exactly. There aren't very many cars around me anymore. It's nothing but open plains on both sides of me. Like a big ocean.

I need gas and a sign says there's a station in a few miles. I'm thinking how great it is to be getting all these opportunities, how everything is just kind of lining up for me these days. Before long, there's an exit that spits me out right in front of a Sinclair.

The sun is almost down when I pull into a parking space out front. I'm absolutely roaring to take a piss, so I lock the doors and jog to the entrance.

There are so many snacks. Weird snacks, snacks you can only find here, but also lots of normal stuff. I figure I'll look after I've taken care of business, so I follow the signs to the bathroom. There's graffiti scratched into the wall in front of the urinal that says "suck dick?" and I laugh at it.

I step out of the bathroom and am about to turn and get something to eat when I notice some tinted glass down the hallway. I can see big thick curtains too, and my heart starts racing. I'm afraid, but I keep looking and I find a door with a sign that says "Lucky Lucy's Casino." My head feels like it's on fire.

And now I'm thinking, oh shit, I'd better call my sponsor, because this could get really out of hand.

I haven't had a cell phone in months. I kept using it to play online poker, so I got rid of it. I thought maybe I'd just get a flip phone, but I knew all my bookies' numbers and I had to stop placing stupid bets. Look where it got me. So, I can't text the guy. I need to use the payphone, but I don't have any change. I just have a twenty.

I peek around the corner to see who's at the front and there's a few people in line. I worry they've seen me looking at them like some kind of creep. Now I'm self-conscious about going to the front. But the casino—the casino would definitely have change.

I look at the door. I pull out my wallet and look at the twenty. You've got this man, I say to myself. You don't have to let this bullshit define you. You're going to go in, get some change, and call your sponsor. Remember, there's no shame in asking for help. You're a fucking warrior every day of your life. Stay true to your inner viking.

And hand to God, I tried.

But the next thing you know, I'm sitting down in a big leather chair in front of a keno machine, and this hefty woman with a big mole erupting from her left cheek is asking me if I could use a drink. And I'm thinking yes, I've been driving a long time. It's hot, even at night. I could probably use a drink. I have a gambling problem, not a drinking problem.

So it's still not really a problem when I have another. But that doesn't leave me with a whole lot of money to play with. I'm doing some mental math about how much money I have in my bank account because I feel like I've got to hit sooner or later and twenty bucks is way, way less than I used to put in these things, so a little more couldn't hurt.

And then, on my last two quarters, I hit fucking *big*. I make all my money back plus ten dollars. So I have two more quick drinks. And, to be honest, I'm not sure why they would serve alcohol right next to a gas station. In the same building, really.

But I don't think about it too hard because I start feeling guilty. I fucked up. I gave into temptation and just blew my wad. The room feels a little hot and I can't really focus my eyes. I think about how the conversation with my sponsor would have gone, and I worry about how the next one will go.

But I make another five dollars on a totally random play and I start having a good time again. I'm having a *great* time, even, right up until the money runs out.

It's always quick like that. I'm out of practice. I should have cashed out a hell of a lot sooner, but I didn't, and that's on me. I'll stop now, while I still have some money in my bank account. I have to.

I have a little trouble getting out of my chair, which is admittedly pretty comfortable and low to the ground. I tell myself the lady with the mole doesn't notice, but she must, because she gives me a stare as I leave that I feel drilling a hole in my back.

I go back to the bathroom and splash my face with some water. I stand in front of the urinal and look at the graffiti that says "suck dick?" again. My eyes have a hard time focusing on it, but I can still read it, so I know I'm not totally gone.

I decide to buy a coffee, a big one, with lots of pumps of fake creamer to cover up my breath a little bit. Walking over to the cappuccino machine, I pass a big refrigerator full of forties and a big rack of wine. And I say hey, I'm not going to drink it right now, but it might be nice to have a little something wherever I wind up sleeping tonight. And who knows where that will even be?

So I grab one of those little cardboard cartons of red wine. Then I fill up a coffee cup. Then I get a few other things that I don't particularly care to get, just so it looks like I'm buying more than coffee and wine.

I drop these in front of the pasty kid working the register. He scans everything then asks for my ID. I ask if he's joking and he says no, he has to check everybody's ID, it's state law. Then he taps a sign on the counter that also says this. I can't really argue, so I fumble it out of my wallet and give it to him. He looks at the picture, then at me, then the picture, then at me, then the picture, then at me. He hands it back and tells me the total.

My debit card is declined.

I ask him to get rid of the gummy worms and try again.

It's declined again.

I ask him to run it as credit.

It's declined.

I tell him to take out the bottle of water.

It's declined.

He says, "Sir, do you need to call your bank?" and I say no, no I don't, and I tell him to just ring me up for the coffee and wine.

My card goes through. I grab the two items and stomp outside.

The sky is pitch dark. It's thick like ink. My eyes can't see through it. I see only a sliver of illuminated highway. It feels wrong, and it makes me want to go back inside to the keno machines to gamble until sunrise. But I have somewhere to be and a long way to get there, so I ease into the car.

I can feel that I'm drunk. I'm not plastered. I'm not sure what the legal limit is because I'm not sure what state I'm in and I couldn't Google it anyway because I don't have a cell phone. I decide to maybe wait for a few minutes before I start driving.

I look at the clock. 7:04. It felt like I was in there forever. I wonder how long I should wait, or if I should just lean my seat back and sleep it off for a little bit.

I sip my coffee. It burns my mouth a little and makes me feel a little more awake. I think to myself, you've got this. You're in control. You don't have to let all that exterior shit cloud your mind. You own your body.

I sip some more coffee.

A second later, my car is running. I'm idling before the highway entrance. I don't remember getting here, but my brain tells me it's too late to turn around now. If Highway Patrol saw me, they'd think that was pretty suspicious. It was probably safer for me to just drive for a while and keep pounding coffee. I'd sober up on the way.

I'm thinking all this and then I'm on the highway. I'm going pretty slow and I don't see anyone else out here with me. I turn to look at the gas station next to me. I'm trying to figure out why it looks different. My foot spasms for a second and I lurch forward. I'm not quite past the gas station when I feel the tires roll over something.

Even through the floor mats, I feel a wetness. I'm so entranced by the feeling that I'm not even kind of prepared for my head to thunk into the roof of the car. I spin around backwards, and there's no guard rail on this part of the highway, so my car flips off the side and slams right into the big green Sinclair dinosaur.

I sit there for a long time.

This was not a very good opportunity.

I get out of the car. I'm shaking so hard my teeth are chattering. I don't think to check for broken bones or anything. I just climb up the hill to the side of the highway to look for what happened. To look for what I might have killed.

This is where it gets tricky.

There is nothing on the road. With no cars coming or going, I run onto the highway for a split second. I feel around on the pavement for the wetness. I realize how dangerous this is and run back down the grass incline to my car.

I examine that, and there is not any blood on, around, or under it. I start to panic. I know I hit something; I knew it was alive.

But there isn't anything here.

My car is smoking, wisps floating out of the front hood. I decide that even if I get in trouble, I need someone to help. I'm a fucked up person and I've done fucked up things, but I want to try really hard to not make murder one of them.

Still dazed, I walk back into the gas station. This time, there are still gummy worms and cappuccino machines and forties in the refrigerators. But it's not right. The interior is completely different. There is a whole row of artisanal snacks that did not exist before, bags of dried snap peas and yogurt covered pretzels.

I feel like I'm going to pass out.

I run for the bathroom, or at least where I think the bathroom is. But now, it's a hallway leading to a Subway sandwich shop. It's closed. I want to cry and I do. Then, I recompose myself a bit and go to the front counter.

There's still a kid working, but he's completely different than the one from before. He's bigger, his hair longer, his skin worse.

"Are you all right, sir?" asks the different kid, before I can even say anything.

"Didn't there used to be a casino here?"

"No," he says, looking at me like the question doesn't make any sense. I'm starting to think it doesn't.

I bolt outside.

I run straight for my car and find it back in the spot I first parked, dent-free. When I look up at the sign illuminating the pumps, I see a big shell. No dinosaur in sight.

I scramble, checking every inch of my car, looking for blood, then for cashout receipts, the wine I bought, anything to prove that I was at a gas station that had a casino inside, gambling away my last twenty dollars. Anything to prove I am not going insane.

I look at my car's clock. It reads 1:45.

I scream and get out of the car. I run back toward the road and crouch down where I think I might have struck whatever it was I think I struck. I need answers. Anything would be better than not knowing.

I get down on all fours, pawing at the ground, feeling for the wetness. I smell my fingers and pray this is all in my head. I'm crying and wiping my hands all over the ground and only feeling dry blacktop. I crawl further onto the road and still feel nothing. I call out, asking if anybody is around. I call out that I'm sorry. I can't hear the sound of my own voice but I keep shouting anyway.

I'm bellowing "HELLO" into the air at what feels like the top of my lungs. I'm praying against all hope that no one is dead at my hand, because I'm just a fighter, not a murderer. I don't want to be a murderer.

And then, just like that, my calls are answered. My shouts are cut short by a great force that rams into me. It moves in jerky bursts, and I am sucked beneath it then split open at the stomach. All my wetness spills out. I smell motor oil and metal and dirt. I hear the scraping of tires and something rolling off the road and crashing into something stationary.

The odds are against me now, and I know that. But it's not a done deal until I'm in the ground. I never give up. I always get back on top. I try to look around and notice my left eye isn't going anywhere, and then realize that's because it's no longer in my head. I've always been an underdog, though. I know I can leverage this into a new opportunity.

I believe all this because I have to. Because this is how a survivor survives. And I do believe it, the next five times the car rolls over me and flies off the interstate.

But not much longer after that.

DeAnna Patrick, mother: This is going to be hard for me.

Carl Devlin, father: He was our first child, one of three before we split for good. I've never heard a newborn scream like he did. I remember walking around the hospital, late at night, when he was finally asleep in the NICU, and I listened to babies cry. Some were loud enough it made my ears ring, but I didn't hear one that sounded anything like him. He screamed like he was trying to force something out.

DeAnna: They ask me where the trouble began, and I can't really begin to answer.

Carl: Neither of us could hold him for two weeks. They thought he wouldn't make it. His screams were terrible, but it was worse when he stopped. His lungs were full of fluid, and he ran a fever so high you could feel the heat coming off him just hovering your hand there. They thought he was going to aspirate.

DeAnna: But he survived. Thank God.

Carl: We had gone so long without sleeping I could barely focus when they finally brought him to DeAnna.

DeAnna: The first few months were beyond hard. He wouldn't let Carl anywhere near him, and every few weeks the fevers would come back. We had ask-a-nurse on speed dial. We counted once; we took him to the emergency room fourteen times before his first birthday.

Carl: Every time it happened, I thought, "This is it. We're going to lose him." His temperature would be 105, 106 degrees, and it happened so frequently they started running CT scans to check for brain damage. When he'd go in the machines, his pupils would stretch out and fill his whole eye.

DeAnna: Babies shouldn't look that miserable. Some days it was hard to look at him.

Carl: The hospital bills racked up and we wondered if it would ever stop.

DeAnna: I don't know if whatever was doing this to him ever stopped. I think it just changed.

Jerusha Naegel, faith leader: The community really rallied around the Devlins. We always do, of course, but most parents aren't tested quite like they were.

DeAnna: They kept bringing us food and diapers.

Carl: We only brought him to services a few times. You have to expect that there will be screaming and crying babies at these things, but it felt cruel to force him to sit through it for hours. He'd come home blistering hot, and it almost always ended in another trip to the hospital.

DeAnna: After two or three attempts, Carl started going by himself and I stayed home with our son.

Jerusha: It concerned me when DeAnna stopped attending services. At the same time, I couldn't help but sympathize. We prayed a lot, but none of us thought he would make it past his first birthday. We did our best to make things easy on them.

DeAnna: Walls of diapers. Canned veggies. The big basement freezer full of bread loaves and chicken breasts. Baby food. Handouts. No one knew how to help aside from dumping half the grocery store on our doorstep once a week.

Carl: There were two weeks where we just kept ordering pizzas. DeAnna wouldn't cook.

DeAnna: In hindsight, I know they were just trying to help, but I couldn't even look at it.

Jerusha: One afternoon, myself and the Jensens were bringing over a big pallet of formula and some other necessities and DeAnna came out on the porch. We said hello, we had some more food and wanted to know where to leave it. I could hear him screaming from upstairs. I don't think Carl was home.

DeAnna: I'm not proud of this, but I was at the end of my rope that day.

Jerusha: I'd never heard her speak like that before.

DeAnna: It just came out.

Jerusha: I'd rather not repeat any of it, if you don't mind.

DeAnna: And then I just went back inside.

Jerusha: We swept some of the powder formula off the porch as best we could, but we ultimately decided it was for the best that we leave.

DeAnna: They only gave food to Carl on Sundays from then on.

Carl: The fevers eventually stopped. He still always ran a little hot, but his pediatrician said as long as it never got above 99.5, he'd be just fine. The screaming lessened, too. It mostly happened in the middle of the night, on days he hadn't been outside or crawled around much.

DeAnna: He was moody, moodier than you'd think a two-year-old could be, but he was manageable. We had good days.

Carl: We both started to relax. It took DeAnna a little longer, but the air in our house felt less thick.

DeAnna: Once, at the very beginning of fall, when he was three, I took him to a park. I don't know if it was the weather, or something else, but it was one of the only times I saw him where he seemed genuinely carefree. He ran straight to a tire swing and asked me, "Can I? Can I? Can I?" Over and over again. He was so small, I was afraid he wouldn't be able to balance, but I was so happy to see him excited that I picked him up and set him on it and made sure he held tight to the chains. And he still didn't seem to weigh enough to really hold it in place, so I straddled it, kind of, and kicked us around in circles. And he laughed, and then so did I, and then both of us said, "weeee!" over and over and over. And he kept laughing, and I realized there were tears streaming down my face, so I stopped the tire swing and picked him up and spun him around in the air and set him down in the sand and tickled him. We were both laughing the whole time, but I was hysterical with happiness. It felt like a miracle. We kept playing at the park until it got dark, and then I took him to a frozen yogurt shop and let him get whatever he wanted. I asked what size, and he said, "Biggest size!" and I didn't care. I let him have it. I let him get all the toppings he wanted. Gummy bears and sprinkles and peanuts and those weird little jelly balls that look like fish eggs. And we sat down and of course he couldn't eat the whole thing, so when he was finished, I stuck my finger in it and dabbed ice cream on the tip of his nose and that made him laugh so hard. He hugged my leg on the walk out and fell asleep on the drive home. I carried him inside and put him in bed with all his clothes on. Carl asked where we had been, he'd called ten times. He was worried about us, why couldn't I answer my phone, all that, and for the first time in my life I just told him to fuck off. Then I sat on the kitchen floor and wept.

Carl: We waited until he was five before we started thinking about other kids. By this point he had started kindergarten, and his screaming fits stopped and were replaced with what I can only describe as angst. He was worried, constantly. His brain seemed like it was always humming.

DeAnna: I didn't really expect to become pregnant, but the vomiting started one morning and I just knew.

Carl: Neither of us expected twins.

DeAnna: I'd catch him looking at my stomach all the time. He'd ask me if the babies were going to be okay. It started making me nervous that he might know something I didn't.

Carl: He kept asking if his brother and sister could breathe in there.

DeAnna: It wasn't just them he was worried about, though. He had an obsession with the end of the world.

Carl: It started with him asking what happens after you die. That's a very normal question for a kid to have at that age, so I didn't think much of it. By this time he was attending services with us, so I felt it was appropriate to explain what we believe about the afterlife, heaven, all those things. Of course that included the return. I tried to make it sound gentler for him.

DeAnna: I wanted to be the one to have that conversation. I don't think Carl ever understood how to talk to him.

Judy Marcus, kindergarten teacher: Ammon's apocalyptic preoccupations were present in so much of his schoolwork. The drawings were the worst. They were everywhere, even in the margins of his alphabet worksheets. I had students complain that I didn't assign enough art that year, and I think it was because I was afraid to. It wasn't the content—angels, flames, things like that—so much as the way they were drawn. Lines scribbled in hard. Explosions of color. Kindergarteners will oftentimes fill a whole piece of paper with one color, but when Ammon did it, and I know this sounds insane, but believe me, it felt hellish.

DeAnna: I never wanted this for him.

Carl: No amount of explaining made it less frightening for him.
DeAnna: I never wanted this for me.

Judy: I just don't understand why a five-year-old should have to reckon with that kind of thing.

Carl: Maybe he was too young. I tried to tell him it was a beautiful thing, that it's the greatest and most perfect thing that could happen to us, and that when it happened, he wouldn't be worried or scared.

Judy: Frankly, I think it's child abuse.

DeAnna: He'd wet the bed every week, at least, from that point on. Just when I thought the screaming had reached an all time low, it was happening every other night. He'd be soaked and sitting up, wild-eyed. He'd tell me, "It's coming." I'd hug him close and put his sheets in the wash and tell him he could come sleep with us, but he never wanted to. We had maybe seven sets of sheets and comforters, and eventually got a rubber mattress, so I'd just wipe it down, put a new set on and tuck him back in.

Underneath the embarrassment was the same anxiety.

Carl: The bedwetting persisted all the way up until fourth grade, when he was ten years old. We'd had the twins by then, and for all of his trouble growing up, they had practically no problems. Healthy, hearty kids.

DeAnna: He stayed panicky the whole time. We took him to psychiatrists, neurologists, urologists. He was poked, prodded and examined by just about every "-ist" in the state. We even drove to Seattle to see someone who everyone on the Internet swore could fix any bedwetting problem. Nothing worked. He kept doing it. When he was old enough to have real playdates, we realized pretty quick that slumber parties were out of the question. And truthfully, he wasn't invited to many to begin with. Other kids knew about the bedwetting and sometimes made fun of him for it, but I think his fear was obvious. I think it scared them.

Barbara Leighton, third grade teacher: His old teachers had expressed concerns about Ammon in the teacher's lounge. Even before I had him as a student, I noticed him walking around the halls looking like he hadn't slept in days. He always seemed lost in thought. It's not something you usually see on a kid that young. He was a good reader, but average at everything else. That was what they all said.

Carl: Even though the bedwetting was still happening in third grade, I still felt like things were going to turn around when he met David.

DeAnna: Sometimes I felt like David was the only person on earth who really understood him.

Barbara: David was strange, in his own way. Moreso in a typical way, at least for a third grader. He was a little withdrawn and liked to draw. Really, it's the only thing he seemed to like. His grades were poor, and he was almost held back in second grade.

His drawings were strange. Let's just say he was clearly watching movies he shouldn't have been, at least at that age. But I saw a change in Ammon when they became friends. For the first time, I'd catch him socializing, walking around the playground with David during recess, having long conversations. Ammon seemed to do most of the talking. I'd only catch snippets of what they were talking about, but the obsession with the apocalypse that I'd heard so much about seemed to have persisted. David listened like Ammon was some kind of village storyteller. The dynamic made me uncomfortable sometimes, but I was mostly happy to see them find each other.

Carl: I was never too happy about their friendship, truth be told.

DeAnna: Carl never liked David. But with the twins around, our son had mostly languished on his own. He was always helpful with them, always gentle. He never picked on them. But until third grade, he was on his own. I tried to find activities with him, just the two of us, when I wasn't in charge of the twins. Carl ... well, he wasn't really trying with him like he used to. So when he first asked if he could have a friend over after school one day, I felt joy almost like that day at the playground. Carl didn't like that he was always talking about horror movies and violent comic books, and for a while I backed him up out of a sense of duty, but the closer David got with him, the less I cared. It became one of our biggest disputes. Among many others.

Carl: I tried to think of his obsession with the resurrection as a kind of piety, but I knew it was the violence of it that he was focused on, and always terrified of. I didn't like that David seemed to think it was cool. But I can't deny that our son seemed to love him.

Penelope Curtis, mother of David Curtis: I wish they'd never met. I'd prefer David had no friends. At least he'd still be with me.

DeAnna: On his tenth birthday, we had a party at a pizza place.

It was just him, David, Carl and me. We left the twins with Carl's parents. He wanted the buffet, so we got there around noon when everything was fresh. He got his own small pizza when we told them it was his birthday, and all the employees came out and sang to him. At first, he was mortified, but when he saw David smile and elbow him, he relaxed a little and started laughing. We gave him his presents. David gave him a DVD set of some of some old TV show he had watched with our son on YouTube. I think it was *Are You Afraid of the Dark?* Which made me laugh because that show used to scare me when I was a kid too. We also gave him a $50 Barnes & Noble gift card and told him he could pick out anything he wanted. It was another moment when I felt like things could be normal someday.

Carl: It was when I was paying the bill that I saw his eyes roll into the back of his head. I asked him if he was okay over and over, and then he started shaking really violently. I ran and tried to catch him, but he tipped over and his head hit the ground hard. DeAnna screamed, and I straightened him out on the floor. David was wearing a button-up shirt and tried to put it under his head like a pillow, but I snapped at him for trying to touch him. I regret that. David started crying and when I touched our son's head it was wet.

DeAnna: He was in the hospital for months. I don't know if it was the way he fell or something else. He was in a medically induced coma for two weeks to bring down the swelling, and I thought this was going to be the end. I wouldn't let Carl touch me the whole time he was there.

Penelope: I didn't like David visiting the hospital so much. I didn't think he was ready to see a friend die, if that was what happened, but he was so insistent, and so, so worried.

DeAnna: They brought him out of the coma eventually. For another few weeks they were concerned that he wouldn't walk, but he started regaining movement in both legs and eventually was able to walk with some help.

Carl: He was completely different when he woke up.

DeAnna: The worry was still there but it had malformed. When you'd say his name, he'd completely ignore you. He was always staring off like he was in a trance, like he was looking at something really intently.

Carl: It was almost mystical.

Penelope: It scared the shit out of me. I hated when he came over. I should have stopped letting him.

Carl: The injury set him back in school quite a bit, and he was held back in fourth grade. David's grades had apparently suffered quite a bit, so he was too.

DeAnna: I didn't know how to help David. He would come to the hospital, with his mother, at first, and just talk to our son. He didn't respond for a while, but David kept at it. He'd bring a new card with some strange drawing on it every time. He'd bring his own magazines and DVDs. One time, he left his entire 3DS collection. I couldn't tell him they weren't getting much use. He'd have done anything to help. He'd tell him about what he was missing at school, about movies he'd watched. I'd seen how they interacted, and I knew that David was not usually the talker.

Carl: He did start talking, eventually. It was David that finally got through to him. Right in the middle of one of David's rants he just said, "Hi, David." He was so happy.

DeAnna: He'd go in and out of that trance from then on. He did eventually get out of the hospital, and only had to carry a corrective cane for a few months. David thought it was the coolest thing in the world. I'd still catch glimpses of who he was before the accident, but he never really went back to normal. I suppose he never really got to have a "normal."

Carl: The end of the world stuff started to really come out during his trances.

DeAnna: When David would come over, all they did was walk around the big field on the edge of our neighborhood, where the land was undeveloped and filled with winter wheat when the season was right. No matter the weather, they'd walk the perimeter over and over again. I didn't try to listen. I was just happy he was moving and lucid.

Penelope: I almost told David he couldn't hang out with Ammon anymore once. I went to pick him up one afternoon, and they were rounding that big field by the Devlins' house. Former Devlins', excuse me. And before David got in the car, Ammon called out to him from the sidewalk. He said, "It's coming a lot sooner than I thought." Then he thanked me for letting David come over. I was scared then, not just because of what he said but because David seemed to understand what he meant.

Carl: It was winter, and that year the ground was frozen solid until April. David was over, and when they came back inside from the field they asked if they could show us something outside. I asked what it was, and our son said it was something he'd discovered that he wanted us to see. He said it was a beautiful thing, and not to worry, it wasn't scary or anything like that. David agreed, and said he knew I didn't like that kind of thing.

DeAnna: I wish I'd said no.

Carl: I was curious.

DeAnna: I can't do this anymore.

Carl: I asked if the twins could come outside too, and he said yes.

DeAnna: This is too much. I'm sorry. I'm sorry.

Carl: So we put on our coats and boots, because it was freezing outside, and I asked if it would be quick, and they said they were pretty sure it would be. I remember being a little annoyed. They led us across the street, to the field, and told us to stand on the sidewalk, and not to come closer. I asked if this was part of it and they said yes. They walked out about 100 yards into the field. I shouted that we could barely see them, and they shouted something back that I couldn't quite make out. Then they started taking off their jackets and snowpants. I should have stopped them then, but I figured it was some kind of joke.

DeAnna: I'm so sorry.

Carl: They looked at each other for a second. Then my son took David's hand.

DeAnna: I love him so much.

Carl: We felt a huge gust of heat come from their direction. It made me sweat. It made the twins cry. DeAnna called out the boys' names and asked what was going on. I couldn't exactly make out their faces, but our son looked calm. David looked terrified, but held tight onto his hand. And then they burst into flames.

DeAnna: I smelled them burning.

Carl: I was holding the twins, and I dropped them down in the snow. DeAnna and I ran toward them, but we were knocked back by another gust of wind that scorched me like sunburn. She kept crawling toward them, and I begged her to stop. I couldn't help but look at the boys. David was screaming, but our son wasn't.

Penelope: Sometimes I wish I could go back and fucking kill that kid.

Carl: I can't talk about this anymore, I'm sorry.

DeAnna: I watched them go black and I couldn't stop it. I just had to look.

Penelope: He murdered David.

DeAnna: All the snow around them melted.

Carl: I already have to live with having seen it. I don't want to relive it for you. I relive it every time I'm in the bathroom, every time I brush my teeth, every time I try to go to bed. Every time I looked at Deanna.

DeAnna: Every time I looked at Carl. Every time I looked at the twins.

Carl: It just stopped working after that.

DeAnna: The fire died out and all that was left were their bodies, smoke pouring out of them. I held Ammon to me even though he wasn't breathing, and I blew into his mouth even when I felt his skin slide away because I wanted him to live. Because even if he was a vegetable for the rest of his life, even if he was disfigured, I needed him to stay alive. And he didn't.

Carl: I made her stop holding him. His body was so hot that she got third degree burns on her arms and chest.

DeAnna: My shirt melted into my skin.

Carl: David's eyes were open but had gone white.

DeAnna: The day after, I told Carl I was leaving him. I needed skin grafts for my burns, and I was about to go in for the first of many surgeries. I told him it was over. He said I didn't know what I was saying, but I did. I told the nurses not to let him in my room anymore. Security eventually stopped letting him in the building. I got out of the hospital and met with a lawyer and moved in with my sister.

Carl: I sold the house and moved to a different apartment. Reporters called my cell phone every hour in the months after. Raising the twins by myself was expensive. I went on some talk shows for quick money.

DeAnna: I hated him for doing that.

Carl: She won't talk to me anymore.

DeAnna: I don't know that I can see him or the twins anymore. They're both six now. Sometimes I'll look at Carl's Facebook and see how they're coming along, but I always close out the second I see them. I don't really know what they look like anymore. It used to be that they reminded me too much of what Ammon looked like growing up. Now it's that they look like what he might have if he were still here. Time stopped for him, and I guess it did for me too. I think about everything going on right now. How horrible it is to turn on the news. How sick I feel all the time. How much I just wish it would stop. I hear everyone say it feels like the world is going to end soon. And I think about my son. And the truth is, I don't care if it does anymore.

Carl: I try to tell myself this was, in some sense, meant to happen. That what Ammon told me it was going to be like might have been true. But when the image of him completely consumed invades my brain, I think about when I told him that the end was going to be beautiful. And I can't help but wonder if maybe I was wrong.

THE A[

A$$OC[

UMNI
IATION

I checked my mail this morning and found a magazine.

I don't subscribe to any magazines.

That was when I knew.

I pulled it out of the mailbox, feeling for an unnatural weight or a foreign substance coating its pages. The back displayed neither my address nor my name. Breath cemented in my chest. I turned the magazine over and examined its front cover.

"RICHMOND STATE MAGAZINE," it blared, in a slick, black font. The text sat atop a photo of a large group of students, masked, demonstrating in the campus free speech zone. The sky was unnaturally blue, with silky wisps frothing at the edges of the frame.

"WHAT'S RIGHT: STUDENT ACTIVISM AT RSU, THEN AND NOW"

"REBUILDING FOR SUCCESS: HOW CAMPUS CENTER IS GRAPPLING WITH A PANDEMIC"

"THE NEW NORMAL: PROFESSORS ON ADAPTING CURRICULUMS FOR AN ENLIGHTENED ERA"

Earlier this week I watched the same car drive through my neighborhood at least three times. At first I thought the passengers were lost, but then I looked at their plates. Out-of-state. Permanent. I watched the street from my kitchen window for hours and kept seeing them pass by, slowing down near my building.

I told myself it was paranoia. I almost believed it.

I stood at the mailbox, reflecting on the past two years. The second I graduated I began executing my escape plan. When the ceremony ended, I sped home as fast as I could, blasting through stop signs and reciting each step out loud. Go to bedroom. Throw pills, deodorant and roll of bills in duffel bag. Drive to airport. Remove and dispose of license plates. Board plane. Never look back.

That was how it went down. I felt like a fugitive throwing my plates in the garbage. It was almost exciting, but the feeling of eyes on my back kept me from enjoying any of it. As I sat waiting for takeoff next to a dozing woman and her husband, my phone buzzed. A new email:

"RSU CONGRATULATES THE CLASS OF 20XX."

I swiped it away and put my phone on airplane mode. I counted backwards from one hundred and concentrated on my breathing.

"Hey buddy, are you alright?"

I was gripping the shared armrest. I hadn't realized. The husband looked at me with a smile disguising mild alarm.

The seatbelt light flashed and the pilot announced our takeoff. I took one last look around the plane and saw no familiar or suspicious faces. I turned back to my seatmate and grinned.

"I'm going to be."

I landed in a town across the country. I won't say where. I checked into a youth hostel, a shared room with a rotating cast of seven other people. I hunted for a new place and washed the same three outfits over and over again in the bathroom sink with a bar of soap.

In between searching for apartments, I lined up a job with a construction company that paid me weekly under the table. I saved. My wad of cash grew. I worked outside. This was what I always wanted; I never wanted to go to college. I thought about the kind of place I'd be moving into. I thought about furniture I was going to buy, hobbies I would discover. For a few weeks, my dread lessened. I began to get comfortable. I began to wonder if they would ever find me.

Right when, ever so slightly, I found myself relaxing, they started calling. The calls came at odd hours; early in the morning sometimes, but more often at nine or ten p.m. At first I passed the calls as soon as the familiar area code flashed my phone to life, but when they started coming from restricted numbers, I found myself tentatively answering.

"Good evening! This is Sarah with the RSU Alumni Association. We'd like to hear a little bit about what you've been up to since graduation!"

This was how it started. As a child, I watched them do this to my father. Every year, I watched him answer the phone only to see all the blood drain from his face. He answered questions I couldn't hear like there was a gun to his head. Toward the end of the call he would protest, pleading with them. He told them money was tight right now. It wasn't really within our means.

But the back-and-forth ended with him whispering his credit card number into the receiver. When he hung up the phone, he sunk into the chair and my mother cradled his head in her arms and made me go upstairs to my room.

Once, my phone started ringing at four in the morning. I threw it across the room, its screen splintering. The sound roused everyone, and lights came on. They shouted, asking what was going on, but I ignored them. I crawled on my hands and knees toward my phone's battered housing, a faint voice emanating from the earpiece as I drew closer.

"Hello? Mr. Jackson? Is everything alright?" I hovered my head over the speaker. "Mr. Jackson?"

I prayed she would hang up.

"We know where you're staying."

Hours later I was on a bus, headed for another town a few states over. I checked into a motel under a different name. I scoured Craigslist for openings and eventually found a one-room apartment with a communal bathroom on the outskirts of town. With no car, I walked to my appointment with the landlord.

"Who'd you rent from last?" he asked, sucking on a thick wad of dip.

"I lived in student housing."

"Uh-huh," he said.

"Do you have a copy of the lease?"

"Buddy, I don't work like that," he said.

We talked. I produced three months' worth of rent from my back pocket, two-thirds of the money I saved. He counted it, then shoved it down the front of his pants. He spat a dark wad on the sidewalk, then beckoned to me.

"Alright, let me show you around."

I forwarded none of my mail. No one knew my address. I bought fifty-pound bags of rice and pallets of canned red beans and prayed no one would reach out.

I pawned my laptop and used the rest of my cash to buy a barebones AR-15 and a prepaid cell phone with no internet. From then on, I only made calls, never taking any. Still, they somehow left voicemails almost every night.

"Hi Mr. Jackson, this is Tom with the Alumni Association. We've been hoping to get in touch with you about how things have been since graduation. We just want to see how the Bengal community is adjusting to their new lives!"

"Hi Mr. Jackson, this is Adrian with the Alumni Association. We understand you're busy with everything going on, but if you could give us a few minutes of your time, we would really appreciate it!"

"We know your fucking address."

My father's mental health deteriorated when I reached adolescence. We moved around frequently and began living frugally. I ate boxed mac and cheese five nights a week and stopped asking what my parents were saving so much money for.

One night, when I was thirteen, a smoke grenade went through our living room picture window, sealing my throat with its acrid discharge. I lay choking on the floor as two men in tactical gear bearing rifles with laser sights stepped through the frame and dragged my father to their feet by what was left of his hair.

They asked him if he was going to pay up. They kicked him in the chest. He nodded weakly and they dragged him out of the room before I passed out.

Now, standing before my mailbox, I pored over every detail of the magazine's cover. I focused again on the demonstrators' signs. Most were at least partially obscured, as if the photographer had instructed them to be lowered. Some, though, stood out amid the noise.

"WE'RE COMING FOR YOU"

"YOUR TIME IS UP"

"YOU CAN'T RUN"

I looked around the block. At first I saw nothing, but then, in the distance, I heard the crunch of tires against pavement. A black sedan broke through the horizon to my right.

I bolted back up the stairs and slammed the lock into place. I wiped my brow with my wet forearm and made my way to the bedroom. I lifted my mattress and grabbed my gun, tucking it under one arm. I made my way to the living room.

They would never let up. They would gather my information. They would ask about my career prospects. They would double-check that they had the right address. And then they would ask the question I had been avoiding for years.

I knew they were on the way. There would be many of them, more than I could handle alone. They would be armed. They would split my door open with a battering ram and pour in, filling my apartment with smoke. They would kick my ribs in and leave me bleeding and penniless.

And while they would get what they wanted from other alumni eventually, they would not get it from me. Not while I'm alive. I will never be interested in making a donation to the Alumni Association.

BEST F

RIEND

Sadie was acting sick all week.

On Sunday morning, while scooping her turds from the backyard, he noticed several spots where the shit, once liquid, dried in a flat mound. Over the weekend he switched her food from whatever he was getting at the gas station to something he bought from an actual pet store. Or, the only one that was open that day.

He wanted to do better by Sadie. She was a really good dog, and sometimes he felt like he was kind of a shitty dog owner. He got her when she was a puppy, and while she was growing up, he took her to the dog park every weekend and walked her almost every day. He was happy and in shape, for the most part, and started identifying with the other thirty-somethings with really nice teeth he saw jog past him on the trail.

What he did not have was their success. He told his friends he was "in a rut" all the time, and for a while a lot of them empathized. But as the years wore on, they wriggled their way into better jobs that paid the rent in nicer apartments, and all he had was his half of the duplex and his dog.

He didn't know if it was too late for his life to start looking up. But when he clocked in at his department store job to spend eight hours folding shirts and stocking kitchen appliances, he usually felt like it was. Most nights were the same: clock out, pick up fast food, come home, let Sadie out, get ripped, let Sadie in, play game/watch movie/read comic book. Pick one. Sadie lost her moxie and started to laze around with him. She gained weight. He told himself she was just getting older, but he knew it was his fault.

He hadn't done anything about it, but on Friday when he got home and he looked at her sagging belly, he decided they both needed a change. His own weight gain was catching up with him, and starting Monday they would both start getting out of the house again. Finishing the bowl of resin and kief he started before work, he decided the first thing to change would be their diets. No more fast food, no more mass-produced kibble.

He researched brands and searched for a pet shop that might still be open. He wanted to use this momentum while he still had it, knowing that if he fell asleep he'd put it off every subsequent morning. It would never get done. Buzzed, he drove across town and, fifteen minutes before closing, bought a giant sack of the most expensive dog food from the only place that was still open.

The next morning he poured some in Sadie's bowl. She looked at it, confused. He, too, was surprised by its appearance. The old stuff was brown and square-shaped, like all the other dog food he'd seen. This stuff was white and chalky and felt weird in between his fingers. But after a few seconds of sniffing it, Sadie took a tentative bite before diving in.

The plan was to give himself one more weekend to sit around being a piece of shit. Then, on Monday after work, he'd take Sadie on a walk. He already felt better giving her the new food, and she seemed more energetic. Even a little cagey, at times. He let her outside more often and she burned herself out running back and forth across the backyard.

Sunday night he was watching *Stargate*. Sadie had been outside for almost an hour, and the sun was nearly set. He paused the movie and got up to open the sliding door. She didn't immediately come inside, and when he flicked on the light, she was on her stomach eating grass, her back legs consumed by shadows.

He called her name and she swallowed another mouthful before running inside. She whined a few times the rest of the evening, but eventually settled down on her bed. He went to sleep a little concerned.

He woke Monday morning to her whining and scooting her ass around the floor, leaving big streaks of diarrhea across the carpet. The smell jostled him out of a recurring dream about having to go back and *Billy Madison* his way through school again in order to obtain his college degree. The smell made him gag so hard a thick gob of sour mucus tumbled out of his mouth.

Mostly, he was worried. She was whining and scared. He jumped out of bed and ran to her, wrapping both arms around her neck and holding her head close to his own.

"It's going to be okay Sadie," he said, scratching her between the ears. She stopped scooting and her tail wagged a little.

He led her to the bathroom and turned the water on, getting it warm but not too warm. He switched to the showerhead and motioned for her to hop into the tub, and she did, even though she hated baths. He detached the head and sprayed the shit from her back legs and tail, lathering her with a special soap he bought last year and never used. She whined a lot and had another accident in the tub, but by the end she was calmer and clean.

He dried her with a towel and led her to her bed, and she laid down and fell asleep. He took the bag of new dog food and threw it in the dumpster in the alley, then put the old stuff in a clean bowl. He scrubbed the floors the best he could but knew he had more work to do when he got home. He called the vet and made an appointment for that evening. They asked for a stool sample and he said he'd get one.

He was an hour and a half late to work cleaning it all up. He worked hard all day to make up for it, but he was already on thin ice with his supervisor and couldn't help but feel he was on his way to getting fired. At the end of his lunch break, he was asked to clean the men's bathroom, an activity always reserved for the nighttime cleaning crew. He did it anyway, without complaining. But while in the stall, he cursed at the clogged toilets and stained dividers and, most egregiously, the lack of real cleaning gloves.

"They're making you clean the stalls?" one of his coworkers, a young guy and a real dumbass, asked, draining himself at a urinal.

"Yeah."

"They must be pissed," his coworker said, zipping himself up and walking out of the bathroom without washing his hands. A small damp spot darkened the crotch of his khakis. The guy smelled like college football practice, sweaty ass and dirt and rain. It made him think of this morning.

He scrubbed coagulated scum off the rim of the bowl. Little grey pieces stuck to the bristles of the toilet brush. There was not enough toilet cleaner, so he sprayed Windex and wiped the seat with a paper towel.

By the time his shift ended it was dark. He counted down the register and wondered how much the vet bill was going to cost. He was on his way out the back door with a cigarette in his mouth when his supervisor approached him.

"Coming in on time tomorrow," his supervisor said.

"Yeah. I'm really sorry, it won't happen again."

His supervisor grunted.

"On time tomorrow."

"Yeah, on time."

"Tomorrow."

When he escaped to his car he sat in silence for a moment, then punched the steering wheel as hard as he could four times. He held his fists to his face, clenching his teeth and making an "rrrr" sound, rocking back and forth. Then he stopped and sat in silence before starting the car and driving home, leaving the radio off.

When he got home and walked inside, everything felt wrong. He called Sadie's name and didn't hear anything. He examined her water and food bowl; both were empty and stained with something dry and white. He flicked the overhead light switch, but the bulb didn't sputter to life like usual. He called her name again. He thought about turning around, but wasn't sure where else he'd go, so he went deeper inside.

There was no shit on the floor, at least in the living room or kitchen. As he approached the hallway leading to his bedroom, though, he noticed a thick layer of coarse dust coating the carpet, paneling and even the doorknobs. A vent circulated air and sucked wafts of it in. He knelt down and wiped his finger across the floor, gathering some of it. It felt like bread mold and left an oily residue.

Covering his nose and mouth with his shirt collar, he grasped the handle of the bedroom door. Before turning it, he stopped and called out his dog's name again. In response, he heard what sounded like her whine, but also sounded like other things softly moaning, close to the ground, by his feet. Her stomach, he hoped.

He heard her whine again, for sure this time. He ran back to the kitchen and retrieved her leash. He ripped a few black trash bags and lined the back and passenger seats of his car with them. Every minute he went to the door and said, "It's okay, Sadie, I'm coming for you, I promise," and his voice became more desperate each time.

He feared what was on the other side of the door, but he knew he had to get her to the vet soon. Nothing about this was right. He wiped the powder from the door handle and twisted it.

The air in the bedroom swirled with the same dust in the hallway. Here, though, it was thicker, resembling pollen or dandelion seeds. On the floor lay a shuddering, wet, copper-smelling mass that he soon understood to be Sadie.

What was less clear is where the other dogs came from.

A great organic mound towered in front of him. Its flesh was specked with matted fur of several different colors and lengths. From this sprouted at least two dozen legs, many broken and bent in opposing directions. Tails wrapped around each other in a gnarled ball. The heads, some quite old, others no bigger than a puppy's, each let out the same human-sounding moan he heard in the hallway. His dog's head lay at the front of the mound, or whatever direction was facing him. It wheezed and took a deep breath before unleashing a whine that made him wet himself.

He watched its bellies rise and fall in ragged fits and starts, heaving all over.

Frozen in the bedroom doorway, he recalled memories with the dog that was now several dogs. Images of picking her up from the pound after his landlady finally approved the request and milked another $150 out of him for a pet deposit; of getting baked and throwing a wet tennis ball down the hallway for her to fetch over and over again, laughing at her tenacity and wishing he could focus like her; of the time she got out while he was on vacation visiting family and his coworker Bryan was supposed to be feeding her, but when he got back he found her on the porch waiting for him; of her face when he left this morning.

And then, of all the nights it was just them, of unresponsive texts to friends trying to make plans, of her hopping up on the recliner with him, even though she was far too big, and him letting her because it's just nice to feel like something gives a shit about you, it's nice when somebody doesn't give a shit that you have nothing going on and your life is going nowhere, to have something to take care of, to experience love every day even if it's just coming from a fucking dog. A dog that he loved, a dog that he failed.

Not knowing what else to do, he called her name. The other dog heads snarled and howled at him but her ears perked up.

"Sadie."

She opened her mouth and hacked, a mist of spores trailing into the air.

He watched the clump of matted tails thump against the floor. Looking in her eyes, he thought of his job and how much he hated it. He thought about having to call 911 and see them take his dog away.

He thought about sleeping alone tonight and how quiet it would be.

He closed his eyes and got closer. Sadie coughed again, and more spores floated out. As best he could, he put his arms around her neck and put his nose to hers. The tails wagged, and she coughed, and he breathed deep. He sucked it all down and did it again and again and again.

⌒

And now when he breathes, it breathes all over.

He wheezes and hacks and sinks deeper into itself. When he's all the way sunk, he ceases to exist. The putrid stench of the room takes on new dimensions and all its senses blaze white hot. There is pain in its guts, churning before bursting through clenched anuses. Dragging itself to the door. Some heads gnawing at the carpet. Hurt leeches from all limbs. It won't survive much longer.

But it has to try.

It has a purpose now, so it has to try.

COP

ING

She had him pinned. He struggled against her knees, pinned at the shoulders as she towered above him with a pair of garden shears. His nose sat crooked on his face, bent seventy degrees to the left and coated with layers of crusty blood. Breath ragged and hoarse, he looked in her eyes, searching for signs of hesitation and finding none.

"Sidney," he sputtered. "Please."

She gazed at him. Twenty minutes earlier she stood outside his house, the one he inherited from his grandfather, ringing the doorbell every thirty seconds.

Once, not too long ago, it was going to be their house. There was talk of a wedding. She began dreaming of cakes. She mostly kept it to herself, a semi-secret known only to her mother and best friend, Lucy. When he was away on business for a weekend, she and Lucy stayed up until three in the morning saving pictures of dresses and drinking spiked seltzers.

There were no rings, but there was a sureness to the way he broached the subject. It made her feel secure.

But security can be breached.

He started staying out drinking with friends, leaving town more frequently for company seminars. They had not yet moved in together, and so she withered quietly in her apartment, telling herself again and again that everything was fine. He was climbing the corporate ladder. He was preparing a better future for the two of them.

One night when they were together, watching *Parks and Recreation* and not laughing, he turned to her and said he needed to talk. He told her he was feeling stifled. That all the talk of marriage was starting to scare him. He told her he wasn't ready, that he still wanted to be able to have guy's nights. He said he felt like he was losing part of himself.

She still loved him. She loved him when she showed up to collect her things a week later and it was all in boxes on the driveway waiting for her. She loved him when she would stare at photos of him dancing with women in clubs late at night. She loved him when she would text him seven times in a day, and she even loved him when he blocked her number.

On the floor, bloody saliva dribbling from the corners of his mouth, his pupils fully dilated, he begged in a whisper.

"Please," he said. "Sidney."

Her eyes welled. She blinked the wetness away. She clicked the garden shears together and drove them through his eye, feeling it bend from the pressure before the tension broke and it popped, like biting into salmon eggs.

He screamed so loud her ears rang. Still grasping both handles, she twisted the shears left to right, digging them down through his skull and into his brain. He stopped screaming and instead released one long, unending gurgle. He seized beneath her body weight. Then, one hand on each handle, she pried the shears apart, like parting the sea, until his head split in two with a tremendous crack. Organic wetness slapped against the hardwood floor, and after a few seconds, his body abruptly slackened.

She had not taken a breath the whole time, and let it all out in a piercing moan. She let go of the shears and they clattered to the floor. She backed up against a wall, clutching her head with both hands and sobbing without producing tears.

Her neck spasmed, then stiffened.

A metallic click.

Her vision went black.

She could still hear herself breathing. A voice, somewhere far off that nevertheless felt like it was coming from inside her head, called to her.

"Sidney."

She gasped for more air. She clutched her own hands, feeling for blood. She felt none.

"Sidney, it's over."

She felt a tugging sensation on her head. She screamed no, no, no.

"Can somebody help me get her in a chair?"

Light roared in. Her eyes adjusted to the sudden brightness. She was in a carpeted office. There were cameras situated in every corner. On a table sat a headset that looked like a welder's mask. A clean bundle of wires protruded from the back and connected to a long, flat monitor. It was black, but powered on.

"Sidney, are you okay?"

There were three men in the room with her. Two of them wore plaid button-up shirts with ties and khaki pants that fit one well and the other loosely. The third wore jeans and a t-shirt. He stood by the door. One of the other two walked around the room, disconnecting wires and jotting notes in a small black pad. The other knelt directly before her.

She remembered where she was.

"Yes," she said. "I'm fine."

⌒

She awoke the next morning with a ripping headache. She couldn't tell if she felt any better.

Lucy told her about the place a few weeks ago. While polishing off a box of rosé one Saturday, Sidney slurred her way through another diatribe about the injustices of her former lover. "He's such a fucker," she said. "I could seriously kill him."

She said that exact phrase many times over the last few weeks. She could kill him for his abuse of trust, for the flippancy with which he ended things, for the way he completely shut her out the second it was over. Lucy always muttered some variation of "ugh, same" in response, but tonight was different.

"Would it help?" Lucy asked.

"Would what help?"

"Killing him. Or, at least, getting to feel like it."

The address Lucy gave her led to an industrial neighborhood that was transforming into a different kind of neighborhood. Mill buildings with shattered windows mingled with a printing press, a domestic brewery, and a suite of office buildings. They all stood together in a row, facing a bright green expanse of young grass across the street.

She parked in the mostly empty part of the office complex lot. She punched in the suite number on a keypad and spoke her name into a metal grate. After a few seconds, a high-pitched beep emanated from a speaker she couldn't place, and the front door slid open.

The lobby was dark. There were several chairs and a receptionist's desk, but they were wrapped in plastic, like bodies. She approached an elevator and pressed the "up" button.

When she arrived at her floor, she was surprised to feel the presence of others. There were at least six people in the waiting room. A receptionist repeatedly took calls and asked everyone if they would hold. Sidney approached her desk with caution.

"Sidney?" the receptionist asked.

She had no idea how she knew her name.

"Yes."

"Right this way."

She was led by the arm through a door. On the way through, she caught several dirty glances directed her way from other patrons. Or maybe "patients" was the correct word.

The receptionist left her in a single office, not unlike the one her psychiatrist from her teen years used. This room, though, lacked the wall full of framed doctoral diplomas and residency certificates. All that hung in this room was a printed piece of paper documenting first aid certification, a business license, and a wide photo of a mountain range in a big box store poster frame.

A man in business casual attire knocked on the door and

entered the room.

He asked questions and she gave answers. She told him about her ex, about the months of heartache and devastation, how she barely felt able to work or even sleep. And when he started asking questions about what might make her feel better, she didn't hesitate. It all started coming out in a rush she could hardly control. She wanted him back, and she knew she couldn't have him. She loved him, but the love existed alongside a growing, burning hostility that sometimes made her stand shaking in place with rage. The things he had taken from her. The time stolen. The memories made rancid.

She told the man, the psychiatrist or whatever he was, that she sometimes lay awake at night dreaming about running him down on the street with her car, or tying him to a chair and sitting in his lap and shooting herself through the back of the head so that the bullet would also go through his head. She felt like a freak.

"People have restrained their desires for millennia," the man told her. "We are now in a place where we can make space for ourselves to be uninhibited."

It was simple, he told her. She would describe the scenario in advance. She would provide descriptions and photographs of the location where it would take place. She would tell them exactly what she wanted to do and how she wanted to do it. If it involved a specific person, she would provide social media accounts. They would collate this data, and her brain in conjunction with AI would fill in the gaps.

"Will I feel everything?" she asked.

"You would be surprised by how much of your brain functions in anticipation of sensation," he said. "You will feel something. I assure you."

⌒

Two weeks after she killed him with the garden shears, Sidney was back in the same office. She sat in a chair (like a dentist's chair, she thought) as the two men from last time set up more cameras and monitors. The same large man stood next to the door, arms folded across his waist, looking straight forward at nothing.

They took her pulse, temperature, blood pressure and oxygen levels. She blew 0.0 into a breathalyzer.

"Are you ready to get started?"

She nodded.

"We had fun with this one," one of the men said as he connected a neat bundle of wires to various ports in the back of the headset. "We spent the better part of a day just getting the lighting right. I think you're going to be pleasantly surprised."

Holding the headset upside down, he turned to face Sidney.

"Last time you exhibited some abnormal brain activity," he said. "We need you to be clear with us about any discomfort or pain you're experiencing. We can't have you seizing with the equipment inserted."

She nodded.

"Okay. Let's begin."

The first time they brought out the needles, she almost left. Old boyfriends had played around with VR gaming headsets, and all they did was hold controllers in each hand and wear a helmet.

This, she soon understood, was different.

Still, she did not protest as they inserted long, thick gauge probes into her flesh. They were connected to tubes; which ones housed wires or carried liquids, she could not tell. They went into each of her limbs, some penetrating veins and others merely entering a few layers of skin. She did not understand the technology before and could barely comprehend it now, but gathered from the pamphlets given to her during her consultation that her movements, or perhaps intentions, were being analyzed down to the nerve impulses. Latency was nonexistent. Immersion was complete.

"We're going to begin circulation now," said one of the two.

She nodded nervously, and a second later her veins were flooded with a heat that made her feel like her whole body was pissing. She closed her eyes, then opened them what felt like hours later. Her vision went static, the fuzzy outlines of the three other men in the room tinted a deep red. From far off, she heard a low voice tell someone to put the helmet on.

Sidney held up her hand, the probes falling around her forearm in ragged wisps. Black dust cascaded from her fingers. A heavy darkness descended upon her, beginning just out of eyesight and slowly eclipsing her whole field of vision. Then there was nothing; no sound, not even her breathing.

"Sidney?"

The voice clanged in her head.

"We're about to put you in."

She held her breath, then slowly exhaled.

"Remember to report any abnormal discomfort. We'll untether you before we let you get hurt."

She waited.

From somewhere far off, she heard the steady pulse of a kick drum. She moved toward it, gliding forward in the blackness until colored lights hissed into view. The kick pounded, radiating through her chest until there was a huge flash of brightness. She slammed her eyes shut.

When she opened them, she was kneeling on the ground, grasping her hair. She looked up to see a small handful of people gathered around her. One woman, wearing a mesh top with no bra, held her by the shoulders and shouted something unintelligible in Sidney's ear.

She abruptly stood, ignoring the crowd looking at her with growing suspicion. She darted through the building, past the bathroom and toward the bar, pushing aside a few patrons and demanding the bartender's attention.

She ordered a 7 and 7 and drank it in three big gulps. She felt the cold against her esophagus, still bowled over by the depth of the realism. Last time she forgot it was a simulation. She hoped to forget again tonight.

She turned around toward the dance floor. Scanning the room, she saw plenty of women that she understood to be his type. He accompanied none of them. Couples gyrated against each other, chopped vocalizations punching through throbbing bass in a tornado of sound. She wondered if she hated the women more than she hated him.

"Can I buy you a drink?"

She turned to see a younger guy in a camo sweatsuit standing right behind her. His hand hovered inches from her shoulder, but when he saw the look on her face, he shoved it in his pocket.

"You just looked lonely," he said.

He looked like the kind of guy that wore silk underwear. His cologne was strong, and a platinum chain dangled around his neck. Beneath all this, he was handsome, and she briefly considered deviating from the scenario for a guaranteed safe encounter.

The guy turned around and held up two fingers to the bartender. She hadn't said anything. Still mulling it over, an opening door in the corner of her eye caught her attention. She turned to face it.

First, she saw two women. One of them picked at the underwear bunched up her ass while the other adjusted a hair extension. They both giggled, faces flush. Once out, they turned around and beckoned to someone.

Her someone.

He slid out the door, looking around nervously before making his way to both women and putting an arm around each. Sidney stared, horrified, as they moved past the bar and approached the dancefloor. He led them both by the hand, and in the center of the room each one dry humped him like puppies. He was uninhibited, occasionally stopping to kiss one and fondle the other.

She felt feverish. Sweat pooled in her eyebrows. The guy in the sweatsuit returned with two drinks and tried to pass one to her, but she pushed him away and beelined for the bathroom.

The door shut, and the music's volume reduced to a low howl. She approached a sink and looked in the mirror. Her pupils were fully dilated. She sunk a fist into her reflection. The glass shattered out of its metal frame and fell to the floor. Someone exited a stall and, seeing the scene, left without washing their hands.

She was told this would be the room. There were only so many places it could be hiding. She first checked the toilet tank, then the garbage can. Running out of options, she stood atop the toilet seat and pushed a ceiling tile aside. She felt around in the darkness until she felt the handle of a black plastic case.

She gripped it and pulled it down gently, steadying it with one hand. She sat down on the toilet seat and clicked it open.

Inside was a battery powered reciprocating saw, the kind he purchased for his workshop but rarely used. Its thin blade glinted in the low bathroom light. Gripping it by the handle, she stuck one of the portable battery packs into the base of the machine. A green LED lit up, and she held the saw in front of her with both hands, clicking the trigger and letting the blade pulse to life. She took her hand off the grip and slid the fingers of her left hand gently across the blade, wincing against the teeth.

Her lips went numb and a searing pain shot up her neck. She arched her back against it, writhing as she let out soft guttural grunts. It felt like touching an exposed wire. Drool pooled at the corners of her mouth.

She prayed they wouldn't untether her.

"Sidney?"

The voice bounced around her skull.

"One more like that and you're done."

She rubbed the back of her neck and grounded herself, rubbing her fingernails against the ridged surface of the saw's plastic case.

"I'm serious. It's not worth brain damage. You need to keep us aware."

She counted her breaths. At ten she moved to a crouching position. She lifted the saw from its case. The battery light indicated it was fully charged.

She didn't need very much time anyway.

She took one last deep breath, then kicked the stall door open. The broken mirror still lay scattered on the floor. Not willing or able to turn back, she shouldered her way out of the bathroom and back into the crowd, weapon in both hands like an insurgent. The dancers gave her a wide berth, and some instantly began sprinting for the door. Those at the center of the floor did not notice and continued slamming against each other.

She stood waiting on the outside of this whirlpool, watching their bodies collide. Then, in the center, she saw him with the same two women. His shirt was completely gone, and he was motorboating one of them, her hands clasped in his hair, face contorted into an ecstatic laugh.

Sidney pulsed the trigger and the saw revved to life.

The woman whose tits he was buried in made eye contact with Sidney, and all the joy drained from her face.

"What the fuck is that?"

He rubbed his face even more emphatically. The woman tapped his head and he surfaced.

"What?" he asked. He followed her line of sight to Sidney. She could see the evening's sweat run cold with recognition, his mouth open but failing to form words.

She stepped forward. The second girl made a break for it, but Sidney stuck her foot out just in time to trip her. She snapped a heel and smacked against the concrete floor. In a swift motion, like she was stealing a horse, Sidney swung a leg over her back and straddled her. Raising the tip of the saw skyward, she lay on the trigger hard before plunging it into the back of the girl's skull.

The point of the blade connected with her scalp, but lost purchase and slid through her ear, bisecting it before it collided with the dancefloor's smooth concrete. Cursing, Sidney again raised the saw and this time drove the blade up through the base of the girl's neck. It went in clean, and the vibration dribbled her head up and down against the ground. The blade would not go all the way through, and so Sidney freed it from the woman's head and turned to face the other two.

Before either could run, she dropped back to the floor and swiped at their ankles, first hers, then his. He collapsed face-first, but she stood in place a moment longer as her severed tendons coiled up through her calves, shredding the muscle, the tension keeping them in place now gone. A moment later they were both howling on the floor.

"Please, please, please," pleaded the remaining woman. Sidney wrapped a fist around her hair and pulled hard,

dragging her up to her knees in front of her ex. He attempted to scramble away but slipped, either from his own blood or the pain. She kicked him back into view and told him to watch.

The woman screamed when Sidney revved the saw again. She held the blade in place against her sternum, letting the teeth shred the fabric of the woman's crop top. She sobbed, saying she didn't understand over and over. Sidney kicked her onto her side and held her with one foot. With both hands, she raised the saw above her head and drove the blade hard through the woman's ear canal, gray tissue foaming and mixing with blood that flowed in great spurts from the new hole in the side of her head. Her tongue spasmed with every vibration and Sidney thought this was funny. She felt the ecstatic relief of a great pressure released and was almost envious as all the shit in the woman's head pooled around her feet.

"Sidney," he said. "Please."

She turned and rolled him onto his stomach.

"No, no, no," he moaned to himself, muffled as his lips kissed the liquor-soaked floor.

She mounted him, thinking about where she'd start. She listened to his chorus of "no"s as she settled on just above the tailbone. The club had cleared by now, the house lights up. The DJ left the same four-bar loop on repeat. She hadn't noticed. She was in it; tasting the blood, smelling the bodies as they voided themselves, the fear in their piss, the dirt in their guts. She had moments of lucidity, but when she did what she paid to do, there was only a single reality, and this was it.

She eased the saw into the small of his back, rocking it to widen the entry point. He screamed, his organs bunching up and wrapping against the blade as it throbbed against his abdomen. She wrenched it up inch by inch, widening the incision into a gaping hole that gave her access to all the rot inside him.

When she was halfway through his sternum, his protestations reduced to a faint dribble. The saw emitted an awful grinding sound and died. She screamed, then rocked the whole machine up and down, attempting to manually split through his chest. She nearly made it through when the blade snapped. He stopped squirming and went soft.

She sat, the bile from his stomach pooling with his blood to form a mixture that looked like coffee grounds. After a moment, she began clawing at the corpse, mourning a job unfinished. Then, waves of pain sent her to the floor before her vision went hazy and her whole body stiffened.

"Get her out for fuck's sake."

The image of her ex and his dead companions flickered. First it went black. Then she only saw their mesh outlines against a stark, gray rendering of the room. Then she saw and smelled and tasted copper again before she felt the sensation of something leaving her. Her body seized again and this time she did not come to.

⌒

They were on vacation. They were renting someone's beach house for the weekend. They had just taken mushrooms and gone to the beach. They were laying in an enormous bed, having just fucked in the kitchen, his arms tight around her. They were smiling. They were telling each other this was the happiest they had ever been. They were kissing each other in funny parts of their bodies. They were making light jokes at each other's expense. They were talking about getting up to get beers from the refrigerator, but only talking about it. They were brushing hair out of each other's eyes. They were talking about the future. They were talking about getting a dog. They were smiling. They were in love. They were in love. They were in love.

⌒

The following week she tried sending him texts. Some were short, others were so long they needed to be opened in a separate window. All came back undelivered, but she typed them anyway, hoping to catch him in a moment of weakness but mostly excising her own thoughts.

It was better than the alternative.

Hundreds of scenarios played out in her head. Maybe he asked Lucy to lunch and she told him. Or she was still signed into her email on his laptop, and he saw all her appointment reminders. Or maybe he just knew somehow, the last remnants of their connection revealing her darkest thoughts to him in dreams.

The clinic called once a week, first asking how she was

recovering, then offered discounts on therapeutic scenarios that induced calm and wellbeing. Bathing with capybaras. Playing with docile polar bear cubs. She passed the calls but listened to the voicemails they left.

She was soon signing into alt accounts to bypass the block he'd instituted on all her social media profiles. She looked at his likes, refreshed his tagged photos all day for evidence of a girlfriend. She looked at the same selfies over and over again, hunting for clues; unfamiliar rooms, unexplainable new guy friends, changes in dress, something to suggest that he'd left her for someone else.

She found nothing.

Until a few months later.

On her lunch break, she drove to a chicken shack and ordered a sandwich. While she waited in line, she reflexively opened his profile on her phone and saw new text beneath his name.

"IN MEMORIAM."

The guy at the counter called for her several times. She stood motionless, eyes welded to the screen. Dizzy, she jogged away from the counter and back to her car, sitting in the front seat and locking all the doors. She read the words again, then again, and again before she searched for posts about him.

A flood of posts from friends and family; some she knew, some she didn't. The one with the most engagement was from his brother. She met him once, when she was visiting their family with her ex for Christmas. He still lived with his parents, his early twenties drawing to a close. He worked at a skate fashion store in the mall part-time and had a girlfriend who was still in high school. She thought he was an idiot, and his voice made her neck tense up the way it did when she heard a fork scrape against a plate. She always left the room when he entered.

More posts, most from within the last hour. As she scrolled, she received a text from Lucy, asking if she was okay. She ignored it, along with all subsequent notifications, and returned to her ex's profile. She scrolled through every single one of his tagged photos, then every photo he posted.

When she was well into his high school years, looking at his acne-riddled face drinking hot chocolate at a ski lodge with his foreign exchange friend Magnus, she realized she was screaming. The sound filled the confines of her car until her lungs were empty. She sucked in an enormous gulp before weeping with her whole body.

Her phone clattered to the floor mat. She lolled to the side, resting her head on the center console between seats and letting tears and snot rain from her eyes and nose. She thought of his smells and his bad habits, his annoying turns of phrase and the way his hands felt on her shoulders. She remembered everything at once.

Shuddering, grasping and releasing her hair, she let time pass. She heard people knock on the glass but declined to acknowledge them. She received voicemails from her boss and ignored them. The sky was going purple when she regained the strength to start her car and drive home.

⌒

The sky is thick with humidity, like it's about to rain. Sidney is wearing gym shorts, a shirt with the sleeves cut off and a sports bra. She grips both straps of a sizable backpack. She's rounding a switchback. All around her, trees tower hundreds of feet in the sky, piercing the cloud cover. Some of their trunks are wider than two cars put together. The Northern California air is warm but not oppressive.

She has a smile on her face.

"Hurry up," she says, and her boyfriend appears, looping around and meeting her. He's out of breath, and she playfully digs her knuckle into his ribs.

"Feeling good?"

"Fuck you," he says, and laughs.

"It's not too far now," she says.

They push through brush. He takes pictures of her in front of a fallen trunk. She tries to climb onto it, but the bark is slick and her sneakers slide off. He gives her a boost and she makes it. She stands atop the trunk like she's just slain it, and, with both fists in the air, gives a great whoop. She crouches and leaps off the top of the trunk. Her boyfriend looks on in alarm and holds his arms out like he's going to catch her.

She lands with both feet on the ground, like an action hero. She rises unsteadily and almost collapses, but he comes to her aid and steadies her. Their eyes meet and she smiles. He smiles back. They kiss and then, for a moment, just look at each other. She breaks the gaze and grasps his wrist and pulls him further into the woods.

They walk and walk until they reach a clearing. Before them stands a modest waterfall. The water flows uninhibited and sparkles in the sun, lapping against river rocks, a radiant blue so piercing she wonders if it could exist anywhere else on the planet. The water splashes over the rocks and comes to rest in a pool that goes only neck deep.

She strips her shirt and shorts and tosses them on a log. She wades into the pool and wordlessly beckons for him. He undresses to his boxers and goes in after her.

They meet. She embraces him and tells him how happy she is to be here with him. They kiss again and again, her hands running through his hair. She wraps a leg around him.

She feels a sharp pain in the base of her neck.

For a moment she is holding nothing. She sees him about a dozen meters away, looking at her blankly, before he snaps back into position before her. She stumbles forward and her head collides with his chest. He puts his hands on her too late.

She makes her way to the log with her clothes. She sits down. He runs after her and sits next to her. When he sits, his ass sinks through the wood for a moment before resting slightly above the log. She starts to feel nauseous. She pushes him away and stands. Steadying herself on a tree, she massages her temples with her thumb and ring finger and holds back vomit.

"Sidney?"

A voice from somewhere above the trees.

"Is everything okay?"

She ignores it and makes her way back to the log. He's still sitting there, staring forward, appearing lost in thought. She sits next to him.

"Are you okay?" he asks. He doesn't touch her.

"No," she says.

She puts her head on his shoulder and pain rockets through her body. She falls forward, onto her hands and knees.

He doesn't move. He flickers a few times, then stabilizes.

The world swirls beneath her. She wretches. Her face feels hot. She knows where she is.

"Sidney, we're untethering you."

She shoots up and whirls around to face him. He is outlined by a red haze. He meets her eyes and stands too.

The world goes sideways. The trees are pulled from their roots. She loses her footing. She tries to fight it. He stays anchored in place and rotates with it.

"I'm not ready," she says.

Whole trunks split. She digs her fingers deep into the dirt and grips the earth with all her might. Everything gives way. All her muscles tense. Electric heat makes her blood sizzle. Saliva foams from her mouth. Vessels in her eyes burst.

He is lost in the blur.

Soon she can't see anything.

THE PRIM

MINISTER

The Prime Minister is dead.

Okay.

That's bad.

That, well, fucking sucks.

There were small storms all week, the week before the Prime Minister died. We knew something was going to happen. We'd been busy boarding up windows and getting the generator ready and getting the food frozen so it wouldn't go bad quite as fast if the power went out.

Whenever we got more than two storms in a row, that always meant the Things That Come On the Lawn would pay us a visit. So we knew things were going to hell and that somebody was going to die.

No one expected it to be the Prime Minister.

There were 25 people before this afternoon and now there are 24. The 25th person was the Prime Minister, but he is dead now. If it was anybody else, somebody nobody likes, (for example, say, Patricia), we wouldn't be so upset. The house is big, and some might even think of it more as a mansion, but still it is cramped. So when someone dies, we've learned to find silver linings. We've learned to "get over it."

"That's the way it goes," we always say, getting dead bodies ready for the Things That Come On the Lawn. We put their corpses out next to the big oak tree in a metal box we found in the basement. We'd draw straws and then the two with the short straws would put on the big metal diving suits that used to be displayed in the living room but are now used for going outside. They were in charge of placing the box and bringing it back later.

None of this bothered us that much. Usually we don't even get sad when night falls and the Things shimmer in through the darkness and drag the corpses away, off the front lawn of our big plantation house and into a hole in time where they were probably having things done to them that are painful beyond human comprehension. By that time all the windows are covered, and when we hear the terrible howl those things make, the one that makes your ears bleed if you haven't stuffed them with cotton balls, as we learned to do, we are usually just sitting around playing Uno, the dead already forgotten.

But because this was different, we all decided to gather in the living room to discuss what to do next.

"We should give him a proper burial," said Patricia, who nobody likes. "We shouldn't let them take him away. He was the Prime Minister after all."

"Are you fucking retarded," said Steve, not asking.

She flinched, like she always does when someone says something nasty to her. Nobody comes to her defense anymore because we have all been individually inconvenienced by her presence or otherwise disturbed by her aura.

But still, Patricia, who was until recently forbidden from talking to or even looking at Janine because her voice gave her terrible migraines, had her heart in the right place. Having the Prime Minister around kept our hopes high.

We did not know what or where he was the Prime Minister of. We all came to the house on our own, running through the woods from different directions, desperately outrunning the hazy, oily ripples that signified the Things That Rip Through the Air were coming to turn us inside out and defile our corpses in some netherworld of unending torment. We were safe inside and so we didn't turn anyone away.

Well, maybe a few people.

But when the Prime Minister arrived and told us he was the Prime Minister, we gave him the best welcome we could. He told us he needed lodging, that he wanted to develop a plan to get this country back on the right track. When he addressed us, it felt like we might be able to get back to normal one day. Perhaps we might be able to stop worrying about the storms that break all your bones and the horrible shimmering Things with translucent skin that crawled onto the lawn every time one of ours died and did horrible things to their bodies.

Steve turned to Patricia in the living room. Everyone avoided eye contact with her.

"If we don't leave the bodies on the lawn they'll come inside," said Steve, flicking Patricia in the forehead over and over again, emphasizing every other word. Her eyes welled up but she let him because he was right, she was being stupid. She was being sentimental. Even the Prime Minister would have to go on the lawn, and even the Prime Minister would have those horrible things done to his dead body; to his dead penis, specifically.

Steve had sealed the deal with that one, even though we all felt a little weird about how aggressive he got sometimes. We thought maybe he wanted to be the Prime Minister. Since no one new had showed up to the house in months, we might have to elect one. We might have to kickstart the rebuilding of this country ourselves. Maybe Steve would be good at it. He seems to have a lot of ideas.

So, we did what we needed to do. We stripped the Prime Minister's clothes, placed him in the box with the gut-stained cardboard lining where all the dead bodies went, and covered him with flowers, at Patricia's request, because we all felt a little bad about Steve flicking her in the head so many times.

Once he was in the box it was time to draw straws. Steve and Max drew the shortest straws. Steve said something about a recount but ultimately decided to accept the job with grace, which we all thought was very brave of him. Usually whoever gets picked totally freaks out and causes a big scene, and we have to all grab them at once and force them into the suit and then push them outside. Max saw Steve was being all noble, and so he decided to be too. It was a nice break for us.

Steve gave a nice speech about patriotism and how he really thought we could do something special, that we might be able to figure out how to beat these things. We all thought it was a great speech and said so.

Then Steve and Max put on the big metal divers' suits to protect them from the shimmering Things if they got too close, which they often did, and hauled the box outside. And as soon as they stepped outside, we saw the clouds darken, and Patricia screamed at us to shut the door, and we did.

Steve and Max banged on the doors and begged us to let them back inside, but we did not. We would wait until the storm was over like we had all agreed upon, with our ears full of cotton. We didn't open the door even as we heard the muffled sounds of crunching bones and sizzling flesh, and, hours later the delighted howls of the things as they crept onto the lawn.

We played Uno over and over again, tagging each other in and out. And when the rain let up and we pulled bloody cotton out of our ears, Patricia turned to all of us and said it was time to elect a new Prime Minister.

SMELLS

Her jaw felt like it was on fire.

Constance stood in the bathroom holding it open with her index and middle fingers, examining her molars. The pain started a few days ago, first appearing when she drank something cold. It originated from the furthermost molar on her right side. It developed into a dull ache that persisted until yesterday morning, when the pain intensified to a hot, throbbing pummel.

She was unable to sleep. It was six in the morning, and for the last eight hours she tossed and turned in agony, sucking on wet washcloths and dulling her pain with over-the-counter lidocaine. Heat radiated from her cheek, and she was sure it was infected. But for all her probing, she saw no cracks or abscesses. There was only the pain that threatened to blind her.

I'm so fucking tired.

She felt the frustration of insomnia broil in her stomach and tried to keep it together.

I just have to make it through today.

When she took a desk job, she expected to feel relief. Until February, she languished on unemployment, a pittance of a check covering her rent and little else. She tried to make do, embracing canned meats and making lots and lots of ramen noodles. The shop next to her apartment always had plenty of both, brands in languages she couldn't understand in script she didn't recognize.

I'll pound coffee until I can leave and then I'll come home and sleep for fifteen hours.

It was a call center gig, a contract job that paid $20 per hour. The last time she worked in a call center, she'd hide in the toilet stalls almost every day to cry and think about doing bad things to the assholes on the phone. But this time would be different. This time she was getting $20 per hour. That meant no more Spam.

Unless she wanted it.

It also meant that in one month, after the trial period ended, she would be eligible for dental insurance. She just had to tough it out.

You haven't ordered out in a few days. You'll have earned it after today.

That would, of course, require her to find something that wouldn't make her tooth act up. At first, she could eat most things comfortably, but on day two, all of her food had to be closer to room temperature. Now everything hurts. Maybe just rice tonight.

You could make some before you go to work. You may as well do something with this time. Then it'll be ready when you get home.

She found her vision growing dark around the edges. Was it finally happening? Her body slackened beneath the black warmth of sleep. Christ, it felt good. Ten minutes would be enough.

Sound exploded. Piano chords like knives slid cleanly into her brain, pulsing waves of lightning through her head. It was the riff from "Bad to the Bone," and that meant it was time to wake up. Her head jerked and her tooth emitted a small radioactive burst.

She put her pillow over her face and screamed herself hoarse.

⌒

Constance took the elevator to the twentieth floor of the cramped high rise that housed a mess of attorneys and accountants. It stopped every two floors and someone new got on. So many people work here. She didn't always recognize them, but today a coworker known for his chipper attitude got on with her.

Ken.

Don't you know Ken? We love Ken. Ken is hysterical! Ken is so sassy. Ken is so on the ball. He's the best thing about working here.

He talked at her the whole way up.

"Runnin' a little late too, huh?" he asked with a big grin on his face. "Yeah, it's hard to get over here with all that construction going on. And they've got the M running express today so it's just a doozy getting over here. I shouldn't have stopped to get this coffee, but my darn dog was keeping me up last night because the neighbors wouldn't stop setting off fireworks. Poor guy. I didn't get to sleep until 1:00 a.m.! You sure look tired today too, so you must know what I'm talking about, right?"

Floor 19 passed and they finally reached the top. The doors slid open and she got out as fast as she could.

"See you on the floor!" he shouted, already beginning a conversation with another coworker, a woman named Patrice who laughs too hard at his jokes and rests her hand on his bicep whenever he says something she finds amusing.

At the coffee bar, she filled a cup with black dark roast. She'd never worked at a place with amenities like this. There was a ping pong table and guys on the sales team rode around on scooters while they tried to close deals. A little jingle would play anytime someone signed a contract, and a different one would play anytime someone made a commitment to a product demonstration. It was vibrant and upbeat, unlike her last customer service job, which was housed on the top floor of a gray warehouse near an abandoned parking lot.

She hated this place more, but wouldn't admit it to herself.

Ken walked by again and made a finger gun at her.

"Break a leg, sister!"

She imagined what it would feel like to cave his head in.

⌒

She took her coffee and made her way to the sales floor. It was the end of the month so there was lots of activity. She knew there was going to be a huddle, and she hated huddles. Being so close to her coworkers was uncomfortable enough on its own, but her jaw was burning. She considered faking her period but decided against it.

At her desk, her computer was already switched on. She took another sip of her coffee through a straw that she placed all the way in the back of her throat. The suction hurt a little, but a thousand times less than if the hot coffee seeped into her molar. She thought about the scene that would start and vowed to be careful when she was drinking it.

She attempted to navigate to the company portal and sign in, but right as she started to type, her supervisor, a big bull of a man with almost no hair on his body save for some thin eyebrows, stormed into the room.

"Alright people let's huddle up!"

Her team consisted of ten representatives, and they were all enthusiastic about their jobs. She got the sense that not all of them genuinely loved these huddles, but they acted as if they did like their lives depended on it.

They all congregated around the foosball table in the back corner of the open office. Two of her coworkers immediately started spinning the rods around, punctuating their movements with "oh"s and "whoa"s.

"Okay guys, can this wait till lunch?" her supervisor asked, laughing, pretending like he's scolding kindergarteners. The coworkers laughed and high fived and hoisted themselves onto the table with their palms.

"Alright, what's shakin'!" one of them said, doing a little drumroll on his thighs. A few people giggled.

Her supervisor went on and on about how it was the end of the month, and he knew they'd all been working hard, but he really thought they had it in them to set a new goal this month. He gave personalized advice to everybody. Drive it home at the end, Todd. Make sure to mention the discount for two setups, Erik. Don't forget about reminding them to check their email throughout the week before the demo, Emone.

When it got to Constance, he just looked at her and told her to keep pushing those dials.

They broke, and she went back to her seat. She got signed in and put her headset on. She was about to make her first dial, but she took a sip of coffee and realized too late she forgot to use the straw. The coffee was room temperature, but even that was too cold, and the moment it made contact with her back tooth she felt a shotgun blast to the mouth. She saw stars and for a moment thought she might hit the floor.

She made a noise at some point, because when her vision cleared several people were looking at her.

"Are you alright?" one asked, the artificial good naturedness replaced with genuine alarm.

She shook her head to snap herself back into the present. Then she nodded and turned back to her laptop. She readjusted her headset and looked at the computer. She could feel everyone's eyes on her but decided to ignore it and just start making calls. Counting backward from 100, she shut her eyes and breathed deep, in and out, until the pulses of pain retreated to the back of her mind.

She picked up the phone and selected a lead from the dialer. It was a highway convenience store in Arkansas. The phone rang three times before someone picked up.

"Hello?"

"Hi! This is Constance, and I'm with —"

She found herself unable to continue. The stench emanating from her mouth stunned her. She could focus on nothing else. It was unlike anything she had ever smelled. With no olfactory reference, her brain flooded her with images: the impacted shit she once heard they pulled out of John Wayne; a freshly split hog; a hospital operating room; the broiling corpse of an invalid.

It smelled like the first thing to ever die.

"Hello?"

Constance slammed the phone down on the receiver and walk-ran to the nearest restroom with her hand covering her mouth. Her supervisor, alarmed, called out to her, likely assuming she was on the verge of vomiting. She ignored him and plowed ahead, ducking a corner and shoulder checking the bathroom door open. Only one other person was inside, locked in a stall. She approached the mirror and opened her mouth.

The gums around her tooth were swollen, but this wasn't anything new. She held her breath while she examined herself to keep any more of the smell from escaping. She looked for several minutes, taking breaks where she would shut her mouth and breath through her nose. She soon tasted something she was sure had gone necrotic. But she couldn't see anything around the tooth.

She switched focus to her uvula and tonsils, checking, hoping, for stones. She had them a few times as a teenager and remembered how disgusting they smelled when she finally worked them loose with her tongue. She couldn't help but smell them every single time. If it were someone else's, she wouldn't have done it in a million years, but it came from her, and that made it bearable.

But there was nothing.

The tooth throbbed. She scrunched her face, ready to weep, and emitted a high-pitched "Fuck!"

A phone clattered to the tile, cracking and sending a few microscopic glass shards into the grout. Two legs with stockings crumpled about the ankles shot into the air, shins connecting with the underside of a stall door. Then, a whole body smacked the ground ass first, seizing like a dying fish for almost a minute before slackening.

She watched it all, frozen in place.

"Oh my god," she said, and the smell saturated the room again. This time it lingered. Each time the smell escaped it took on new dimensions. She was sensitive to all of them because it was her smell, but even still, its power left her weak. Her esophagus contracted, then bulged as hot bile rocketed up her throat and out her mouth.

Dazed, entranced by pain, she grabbed a handful of paper towels and wiped some chunks off her sweater. She dropped the wettest ones on the ground and covered her mouth with the remainder. She was drenched with sweat. Her cheek scalded her through the paper towels and she pulled her hands into her sleeves to protect them from burns.

She wondered if she was dying. Then she wondered if the girl in the stall was already dead. She became lucid long enough to realize she needed help.

She was back in the office now. Across the room, her coworkers were bunched in a corner together. They hadn't noticed her yet, talking all at once, in different combinations. It felt like time slowed as she listened.

"She completely spazzed out for a second. I thought she was going to pass out."

"Is she, like, fucked up?"

"I don't know what the fuck she ate but oh my god, the smell that came out of her mouth was like ... I don't even know, I can't even describe it. It was that bad."

"Where is she?"

"If she doesn't book a demo today, we're fucked."

"All these new hires fucking bail because they get too burnt out right away and can't handle staying a few extra hours for one week of the month."

Suddenly she was in front of them, and they all shuffled uncomfortably in their seats before they really got a good look at her. Their expressions shifted from discomfort to alarm.

"Sweetie, are you okay?" a woman from the neighboring team asked.

She mumbled beneath her hands, which formed a tight seal across her mouth. Even still, the smell leaked. It grew more concentrated every second it was in her mouth.

"I can't hear you, can you move your hands honey?"

She tentatively dropped a hand.

"Please somebody help me," Constance said, pleading with the woman from the other team.

The woman staggered for a moment. She wobbled her limbs in place, standing erect but unstable. Her eyes were rolled all the way back into her skull, and the whites went dark and then began to fill with blood. Her gyrations became violent spasms, and foam billowed from her slackened jaw. The foam became thick and viscous, streaking red as it poured from her mouth in a slurry of tissue. She involuntarily coughed, spraying gobs of whatever was breaking down inside of her in all directions.

"Please," Constance said to anyone. Her coworkers smeared into blurs of color, her vision only capturing motion. She felt herself collapse like a detonated building, sinking down to the floor right leg first, emitting a loud moan. Her head splashed against the carpet, and she kept groaning. The horrible ringing in her ears was her only sensory connection to the office, and still she sensed no bodies moving. Everyone was frozen in place.

The smell.

Her mother was a clean freak. When she was in middle school, she was assigned weekly chores, and one of them was bleaching the bathtub. She scrubbed the porcelain every Sunday evening with a sponge. They were always out of face masks. Her mother used them all cleaning everything else, even bleaching the tub other days of the week. The smell of bleach singed her nostrils and she had bloody noses that persisted until she had her nose cauterized in college. When she got her own apartment, she started cleaning with vinegar. She was quick in the shower because the feeling on her bare skin reminded her of the smell.

She smelled nothing now, but the burning was back. It was worse than ever. A pool of blood formed under her resting head, and she ascertained it must be coming from her nose. Gushing in torrents that pulsed with the beat of her heart. The speed with which it poured made her head even lighter and finally, mercifully, she passed out.

Her mouth was open and she continued to breathe. And when the police kicked down the office doors later that night, after loved ones called worried because no one who works there returned their calls, the smell made its way outside and did its work.

⌒

The city was devoid of life.

The streets were littered with the broken remains of police barricades and military vehicles.

Constance wandered.

Night blanketed downtown and she lay underneath the stars, wondering if this was her destiny, and what destiny she might be fulfilling. She couldn't smell anymore. Not like she used to. She tasted with her fingers. Everything was clearer now.

There were no birds or crickets. The grass in the parks lay brown in brittle piles. She felt the sweetness of decay in her bones and accepted its place in her new life.

She returned to her workplace and climbed twenty flights of stairs. In the first days after the smell escaped, she felt tremendous guilt for killing her coworkers with her illness. If you could call it an illness. She reached the big metal door that served as an alternate entrance to the reception area.

When she opened it, a watery blood syrup leaked like melting snow onto the concrete before her.

She never went back.

She was unsure how long she'd been alone. She'd lost count of everything; how many days it had been since she heard a bird caw; the last time she breathed fresh air; the last time she heard a voice other than her own.

And still there was the pain. The tooth kept it from fully escaping, she came to understand; the smell was nothing close to what lay beneath it.

But today was the day.

She made her way back to the maintenance shed in the public park where she slept, a rare place not tainted by gore. She spent nights in here with no light other than the moon; the dead buildings emitting no more pollution. There was rain in the days before the smell, and the heat that followed allowed her to leave the door open at night. But the heat was leaving and soon she would have to begin the hard work of surviving a winter with no one else around. She did not feel prepared.

Her tools were on a dusty shelf. She picked up a pair of pliers and clicked the conjoined halves together. She tested their grip on an eye tooth, and satisfied, felt the molar with her tongue for one last time. The consequences of this no longer mattered. All that was left was the blinding pain and the burning and the memory of the smell.

She put the pliers in her mouth and felt the serrated metal with her tongue. The teeth gripped the molar with an affirming steadfastness.

She began to pull.

Roaring light rocketed into the sky from the shed, from her mouth, until it died in an atomic burst. When it was over, the sky un-split itself. She felt much better.

WITC

The boy was splayed on his back, flies buzzing in and out of his head in lazy figure eights. He clutched a toy pistol in his left hand, fingers stiffened around the grip. There was no blood on the ground beneath him, but the exit pattern of a bullet emphasized itself on his right temple. He wore a cowboy's vest, child's Levi's with an elastic waistband and a t-shirt that said "Who's the Man?"

Callum and Jacob stared at the body for a long time, processing it. They were hunting a rabbit they caught sight of at the other end of the park. They chased it toward where the park met with the nearby woods. A huge storm drain sat down at the base of a creek that ran through this part of town, filled with weeds and garbage left behind by drunk high schoolers. The rabbit leapt down into the ravine, and both boys pursued it ravenously, ready to unload on it with their BB guns.

They lost sight of the rabbit in the brush, and found themselves dejected at the mouth of the drain when they noticed a shoe sticking out from the rush of water.

They pulled at the shoe and found it connected to a body. Both climbed into the drain's opening and crouched next to him. They repositioned him in a way that, at the right time of day, would allow a sliver of the rising sun to illuminate his face.

They marvelled at the boy's features, slightly bloated, his tongue swollen and partially protruding from his mouth. Aside from the blood, he was not dirty—he was placed here with some care.

After consideration, Callum exited the drain for a moment. He collected two sticks and handed one to Jacob, mumbling something about how they shouldn't touch it with their bare hands because they might get AIDS.

Neither of them smelled an odor.

"This is messed up," said Jacob, and Callum nodded, twisting his stick in his hands like he was about to cook a marshmallow.

"What do we do with it?" asked Jacob.

"Leave it, I guess," said Callum.

Callum reached for the boy's hand and pried his fingers away from the toy pistol. They were stiff around the grip and remained in the same position once it was freed. He examined it with care, taking in all of its angles and absorbing its image. He shoved it into his jacket pocket and slugged Jacob on the arm.

"Let's go," he said. "We'll come back tomorrow."

"Wait," Jacob said. "They'll find him."

Callum thought about that for a moment, then elbowed Jacob, a request for help. The two lifted the boy's body by his feet and armpits and carried him back toward the bush. They parted the branches and placed his body within, covering him with scattered leaves and twigs. They made sure his feet stayed covered.

They scurried up the incline and looked down at the storm drain, trying to see if any part of the boy's body was visible.

As far as they could tell, it wasn't.

"I have to go home now," Jacob said.

"Me too," Callum said.

It was late October, and it would be dark soon.

They walked toward home together, not saying much. When the houses were about to give way to apartment complexes, Jacob silently said his goodbyes and turned left, heading toward his family's two-story stucco.

Callum continued for several more blocks until the sky went all black. The stars were covered by a thick blanket of clouds, and when he finally reached his mother's apartment, Callum sat outside for a moment longer. He listened as the downstairs neighbors argued, and wondered if his mom would be off early tonight. He wondered what was in the freezer that he could make for dinner.

⌒

Jacob sat with his parents on the couch, watching television and eating dry roast beef off a TV tray. The milk he drank was on its last legs and would be spoiled by the end of the week. He made a mental note to inform his mother of this, and hoped she would listen. He still liked milk.

He wanted to leave the living room and continue reading the fantasy novel he checked out from the school library, but his parents insisted that dinner time was family time. Television didn't offer him much. He especially couldn't see the appeal of the really old show about all the people who hung out at the same bar that his parents loved so much.

The episode was about to end, the telltale swell of music before the credits signifying to Jacob that he was soon to be free. His parents would likely ask him questions about his day, and the truth was he didn't want to think about it too much. He had done his best to keep thoughts of the boy at bay, attempting to recall as many plot details as possible from his book ever since he got home. He scarfed down the rest of his dinner, ready to make his escape.

The show had ended and the news began to play. Jacob asked if he could be excused. His father waved him out of the room.

As he was on his way out, an anchor's voice cut violently through the room.

"The search for a Lakeside boy has turned up no new evidence."

Jacob paused.

"Five-year-old Charles Davis was reported missing two days ago by his parents, Rhonda and Carl Davis, after he disappeared while playing in the family's front yard on Emerald Street."

On screen, a married couple stood in their front yard. There were Halloween decorations all over the porch. Then a picture of

Charles flashed on the screen, and Jacob nearly dropped his plate. He darted out of the room with no thought for maintaining his composure.

He sat on his bed for hours, contemplating the juxtaposition of the boy's face on television and the puffy, lifeless one he discovered in the storm drain. If Jacob hadn't thought about the boy much since returning home, he was all he could think about now. He considered telephoning Callum, but decided against it. The police might already be listening.

He sat in silence for hours, completely unaware of the time, turning the image of Charles Davis' face over and over in his mind until exhaustion took hold and he passed out, still in his school clothes.

He dreamt of drowning in shallow water, his face held into a puddle by an unseen, impossibly strong hand.

⌒

Callum sat on the kitchen counter, eating a bologna sandwich, staring intently at the linoleum. His eight-year-old sister, Megan, walked in and asked what he was doing. "Did you do your homework, Meg?" Callum asked.

"I don't have homework today," Megan said.

"Did you take a bath yet?" Callum asked.

"I don't take baths anymore," Megan said. "I take showers."

Her feet were stained black with dirt, and Callum wondered in passing if she was at the park that day too. He imagined her skipping around, coming across the storm drain, looking into its recesses and seeing, just barely enough to be visible, the protrusion of a hand in firing position. He shook the thought from his mind.

"Go take a bath, Meg," he said.

"Mom's not home and I don't know how to turn the water off," she said.

"Yes you do," Callum said. "You just push the handle down."

Megan groaned.

"Go take a bath."

She stomped out of the room.

Callum hastily ate the rest of his sandwich and retreated toward his room. The sound of running water bubbled from behind the bathroom door.

"Don't just run the water, Meg, take a bath," Callum said.

He heard Megan groan, followed by a splash.

He stepped into his bedroom. The walls were lined with posters of athletes he didn't know or care about, but whose images he displayed to cover the flaking paint, gifts from relatives who he hadn't seen since he was six. The rest of his room was mostly bare. His BB gun leaned against a far corner, a plastic container of ammunition on the floor next to it.

Callum opened up his backpack and pulled out his sixth grade math textbook. His eyes quickly glazed over at the parade of numbers and letters, and his thoughts eventually returned to the body.

He looked familiar, that was for certain. Their town wasn't all that small, but compact enough that the same faces made regular appearances. He wondered where he had seen this kid before. He thought it could be someone's younger brother, but had no idea whose.

He felt a vague disquiet wash over him, an unease at his willingness to hide the body rather than tell the police or an adult. He felt entranced, almost as if something outside himself compelled him to hide it so he could visit it again. That urge superseded all of Callum's anxiety, and when he finally shut his textbook at 11:30, none of his homework completed, he resolved to return the following day.

⌒

Rhonda Davis sat in her bedroom with the lights off. She did not cry; she found herself incapable of doing so today.

She thought about her son, Charles, and how Halloween was coming up. In the last few years it became his favorite holiday. He loved helping her put up the scary decorations, and especially loved to ring the special doorbell that made a cackling witch sound when you pressed the button.

She wondered if she would be able to take him trick or treating a few days after. If he didn't come home by then. She'd have to call the neighbors and let them know in advance they were coming around. Everyone was being so nice to her these last few days. She was sure they would oblige.

Her husband was out, at the grocery store. He'd been there for over three hours now. She assumed he was really at a bar, which was fine with her. Charles wasn't back yet, so there wasn't much of a reason for him to be home. Not after the last few months.

The first two days he was missing, all she could assume was that he had died. She found herself incapable of imagining her son's body, having to identify him days later at the county morgue, or worse, never finding him. That thought almost scared her more, so she decided to remain optimistic instead.

Her husband told her she was delusional, that she needed to start to accept the "reality of the situation." She wasn't sure what he meant by that. The reality of the situation was that Charles was missing, and that he probably was somewhere close by, just like the police told her when he was only missing for a few hours. He would eventually turn up and everything would go back to normal soon. They would have to take him to the doctor to make sure he was alright, and everyone would think they were terrible parents for letting their child run away, but at the end of the day he would return. Everything would go back to normal.

Since Charles left, Rhonda dreamt every night of her son running through the forest, pursuing some sort of wild animal. His favorite movie was *Jungle Book*, but the closest thing he had to that kind of costume was the cowboy vest and toy pistol his grandmother purchased him for his fourth birthday. Still, he pretended to be Mowgli, picking berries and chasing the animals in his imagination.

In her dream, Charles captures the animal, (different every time, most recently a sparrow) and instead of killing it, holds it, petting it gently and subduing it. This was the boy she raised, one who was loving and kind, one who did not want to hurt anyone or anything. Her husband was often put off by his nature, insisting that he toughen up. But the world, Rhonda thought, was too cold, and so was her husband. She saw how Charles lit up any room he was in and knew he was going to make a difference.

∩

It was exactly as they left it. Charles' skin turned a slight shade of purple overnight, and more color drained from his face, but he was otherwise in the same shape as yesterday.

"I think his name is Charles," said Jacob.

Callum nodded.

"Where'd you hear that?" he asked.

"Watching the news. His picture showed up," said Jacob. "If they find us looking at him, do you think they're gonna think we did it?" asked Jacob.

"I don't know," said Callum. "I don't think so."

"How do you know?" asked Jacob.

Jacob grabbed a long branch and used it to push the boy's head to the side. It didn't move much. He examined the bullet wound. It was cleaner than expected. In the movies he had seen, getting shot in the head meant the whole thing exploded. This wasn't like that.

"Why would somebody shoot him?" asked Jacob.

"I have no idea," said Callum.

They gingerly pushed the body back behind the bush, covering it again and darting up toward the park, this time with more urgency.

When they were several blocks from the park, Jacob asked:

"Should we tell the police?"

Callum stopped walking.

"You said so yourself. They might think we did it."

"Why did we move him?" asked Jacob.

"I wanted to get a better look at him," said Callum.

Jacob wanted the same thing, but did not say so.

"I'll see you tomorrow," said Callum.

"See you," said Jacob.

∩

Hey there, kiddo.

Hi.

What's that you're playing with?

A gun.

A real one?

No.

Are you gonna shoot me?

No.

Good. You wouldn't shoot a lady, would you?

...

What's wrong?

I'm not supposed to talk to anyone when I'm alone.

Where's your mom?

Inside.

Then you aren't really alone, are you?

Maybe.

I'm your neighbor. I live just down the street.

...

I just moved here. Do you want to explore the neighborhood with me?

...

It's not polite to ignore people.

Sorry.

It's okay. What do you do for fun around here?

I just play.

Playing is fun. I'm pretty good at playing.

...

Why don't we take a walk? I'm sure your mom could use a break.

...

I can get you some ice cream too. I think I heard the truck earlier.

...

Any flavor you want.

...

What do you say?

...

Come on, let's go!

Okay.

⌒

Today was Halloween. Most kids were wearing costumes. Jacob was wearing a Scream costume his parents bought him from the mall. When you squeezed a pump inside the costume, blood drained down the mask's face. It was a little big on him, and his teachers made him take the mask off during class because it was distracting. Callum wasn't wearing a costume.

School was cruelly long. The classes dragged on for an eternity. The ritual of going to the creek and visiting the body was happening daily now, their need to see it compulsive. They messaged each other throughout the night, reassuring each other they hid the body well, that no one was going to find it.

The bell rang at 3:00 and the boys were already finding each other in the hallway. They couldn't waste any more time.

When Callum and Jacob returned to the creek, they felt a new vibration in the air, a palpable excitement. Trying to appear nonchalant, the two walked in the direction of the storm drain.

As the ravine came in sight, Jacob sucked air through his teeth. Callum swore.

A dozen boys and girls, all from their middle school, were crowded around the bush where they last left Charles' body. It was pulled crudely from its covering, exposed to everyone. His cowboy vest had a new tear on one flap.

One of their classmates noticed them and shouted out. "You're never gonna believe what we found."

The two eased toward the ravine, skidded down the incline and composed themselves as best they could.

"What is it?" asked Callum.

Jacob said nothing.

"It's a dead-ass body, that's what," said their classmate.

The group giggled.

"Isn't it messed up?" said another.

The commotion ignited something in Jacob, an almost vengeful pride.

"We found it first," said Jacob, suddenly.

"Liar," said their classmate. "We were climbing around down here after school and Marcus found his shoe sticking out of the bush."

"He used to be in that drain," said Callum, feeling the ferocity as well. This was their discovery, and it was compromised.

"You're such a liar, Callum," said someone.

Callum reached into his backpack and produced the toy pistol.

"He was holding this," Callum said.

Jacob didn't realize he still had it.

"Give it to me," their classmate said.

Callum shook his head.

"I said give it. I wanna see it."

Callum put it back in his jacket. His classmate charged him, knocking him into the shallow water and landing blows to his face and chest. Callum struck back, the crowd around them screaming. He stood up and shoved his classmate against the other side of the ravine, knocking him to the ground next to Charles' body. His foot grazed the corpse's abdomen, and the desecration enraged Callum further. He leapt up with a kick to his classmate's shins.

The fight lasted for what felt like hours. The screaming of the children did not stop until a voice shattered the commotion.

"What are you doing down there?"

They all looked up simultaneously. Two police officers stood at the edge of the ravine.

"Break it up," said the other cop.

The crowd shifted toward the body simultaneously, like a school of fish, attempting to hide it from the officers' line of sight.

"What's down there?" asked one cop. The other began to descend the incline.

"Move out of the way," he said.

The children reluctantly parted.

⌒

Within minutes, police swarmed the area. All the children, the ones who didn't immediately run away, sat above the ravine staring at the clamor below, awaiting questioning. The presence of authority lent reality to the situation, and the acceptance that the body they found was, in fact, real, came to all of them. Some of them cried.

Charles' body was covered by a tarp, awaiting the coroner's arrival. Photographs of the scene were taken, and cops scoured the brush for evidence. They wouldn't find any.

One officer approached the group.

Another child burst into tears.

"Why didn't you tell anyone?"

The group remained silent for a moment. Callum suddenly spoke.

"I'd never seen anything like it before," he said.

The officer shook his head.

The fear of punishment was beyond them.

Eventually, Charles' body was pulled from the ravine and loaded onto a stretcher. Parents came and picked some of the children up. Jacob was carted away by his supremely angry father, leaving Callum alone, watching.

"Go home," a cop said to him.

He remained for a moment longer, his eyes glued to the bush where Charles was once hidden. He hadn't told anyone he and Jacob discovered the body days earlier. He wasn't sure if anyone else repeated what he said when they first found the body. He didn't care.

He watched as the ambulance drove away with its lights off.

He started on his path home.

⌒

The doorbell rang. A witch cackled.

Rhonda Davis sat alone in the living room. She could hear about four kids rustling outside. The lights were off except for a few candles. She had not moved from the couch tonight.

Her phone buzzed again, a total of eight times before it stopped and turned into a notification on her phone.

59 missed calls.

Then:

16 voicemails.

She savored the silence. She shouldn't have answered the phone a few hours ago, when the police called and told her they found Charles and that they were very sorry, but she needed to come down to the station.

Her husband was with her, and he asked what they said. She said he needed to talk to them because they were obviously mistaken and it wasn't good for her to have her feelings played with like this. He took the phone, and then a few minutes later, he was on the floor. She stepped around him and into the living room.

At some point he got in the car and drove off. This was good. She wanted a little alone time. She wanted time to think about the next steps.

The doorbell rang again. The witch cackled again.

He wanted to wear his costume. Every year, he just wanted to wear the vest. She made him put on a winter coat every year and it would cover up the vest and he didn't care. All he wanted was to wear it. She tore the house apart yesterday looking for it before remembering he was wearing it when he went missing. His room was still a wreck. Maybe she could clean it up tonight.

The phone buzzed again. 59 became 60 and 16 became 17.

She didn't even have any candy this year.

She felt mucus down her nose, and when she rubbed her eyes to clear them they felt raw and flaky. She remembered suctioning Charles' snot from his nostrils and how he'd stop crying the second his sinuses cleared. She needed to be cleared.

61. 18.

62.

63.

Rhonda put a throw pillow on top of the phone.

She couldn't keep it inside anymore and she let it all out until she couldn't breathe.

She stained the house with her sorrow, the walls forever glazed

with its nicotine patina.
  The doorbell rang.
  The witch cackled.

BON

ᗡING

"Wake up."

No light shone through the bedroom windows. When the police would come, later, the mid-morning sun would bore itself deep behind his eyes, heating the folds of his brain until they were sticky with dew. Now, a matte darkness shrouded him, but not so completely that he couldn't see the thick silhouette of his father standing in the doorway.

He arose. He knew this day was coming, had known for years. He didn't know when, and neither did his father. But the knowledge sat with them at all times, a fourth family member at the dinner table. At baseball games, school plays, birthdays, heart-to-heart conversations; it was always present, the gnawing dread of knowing what needed to be done.

They moved through the house, careful not to wake his sleeping mother. She would not understand this, the necessity of it, what was at stake. The two of them weren't sure they did either, at least not fully. As they neared the sliding glass doors that led to the backyard, he wondered how she would feel in the next few hours, what thoughts would go through her head when she saw what he had done.

He stuffed those thoughts down.

Now, outside, the door clicked into place, the motion-detecting light switched on, he saw his father's work: a wide circle, burned into the lawn. He looked deeply at his father, visible now, and saw the same man he'd seen every day: the kind, doting American History teacher, always quick to understand and generous in offering comfort. His outward stoicism belied kind eyes, and sadness over what they were about to do beneath them.

"Once this starts, we don't stop for anything."

The night before he started third grade, his father asked him to come into the living room. His mother was out picking up a take-and-bake pizza, and they sat alone on the couch, the warm glow of lamplight making him feel safe. His father told him they needed to talk, that he wasn't in trouble, but that this wasn't going to be a nice talk. He told him it was time to tell him the truth about what happened to grandpa.

"I need you to know that I love you."

They stepped into the circle.

His father lunged forward, throwing him to the ground and pinning him with both knees on his arms. A torrent of pain as a fist sank into his nose, his vision filling with exploding stars as blood and snot cascaded from his billowing nostrils. Another blow sent the resonating crunch of broken facial bones sounding into the night air. It hurt so much he couldn't even scream. His father mercifully rolled off him.

"We have to do this. It hurts tremendously and you will carry it with you for the rest of your life, but it needs to be done," his father had said on the couch.

He thought of how the pizza tasted after that conversation, after he learned that in just five years, he too would have to kill his own father. He thought about how he wept, how his mother teased him for years for crying over not wanting to go to school, and how his father, in his eternal kindness, simply placed his hand over his.

With one last look at the night sky, he shot up from the ground and found his father's form. He charged him, sending a knee into his stomach before wrenching both thumbs deep into his eyes, the slick, oily feeling both disgusting and exhilarating him.

Father abruptly leaned into son's thumbs, sending them deep into his sockets. Caught off guard, he pulled them loose and was quickly met by the deafening crack of his father's skull against his. Staggering around, senses in chaos, they flailed blindly before their hands met. Like dancers they fell into each other, then began to claw. They tore strips from each other's flesh, broke fingernails and left them embedded in limbs. In between they landed punches, kicks, slaps.

He let out a massive cry. Lights turned on in nearby houses but neither noticed. His father breathed raggedly, his movements drunken and erratic, his brain beginning to fail as he swiped aimlessly at his son. Weeping, he grasped his father's hair with his fist and dragged him to the fence. With everything left in his body, he forced his father's face into the maroon planks of wood, again, again, until his father's body went limp.

Vomiting, falling to his knees, he moaned in agony as the night sky effervesced into orange, the deep red of the sun boiling through the clouds. Before collapsing to the ground, he caught a glimpse of his mother watching silently from the window.

MAR

WILLIAM BLAKE: *[offstage]* Those who restrain Desire do so because theirs is weak enough to be restrained; and the restrainer or Reason usurps its place and governs the unwilling.

— I guess it was around 12:30 in the morning when we went down to the Depot, the one on Washington Ave., and I said, you know, hey, why don't you get us some drinks, I'm gonna go out back and have a smoke real quick.

— I don't care, baby, just get me anything. I'll be out in the parking lot.

— So she says okay, and I just needed to step outside and catch my breath and think for a second. I could feel myself kind of, I don't know, giving into it I guess. All I could think about was getting a plastic bag over her head. That was always how I wanted to do it, you know, I liked the idea of seeing her ... I guess him, whoever, kinda suck in and not have anything to breathe out.

— The lights in this bar make me feel woozy, and I look at the Coors sign and let the neon fill my vision until it's almost the only thing I can see.

— You okay, sweetheart?

— I just need two Coronas.

— Then what happened?

— She came outside looking for me and I said we should go back to my place and she said okay.

— He's at the payphone calling a cab and I can hear his nickels and quarters falling into the slot from across the room and I know I'm not going to fuck him, not tonight or not ever, but I'm still going to go home with him because I think he has something planned for me and I'd like to find out what it is.

— We didn't say much the whole cab ride back to my apartment. I didn't touch her and she didn't touch me. Sometimes she'd look me in the eyes like she was trying to understand what I was thinking about. When we got in, she sat down and asked for a drink and I knew it was my chance. So I went to the kitchen and stuck a grocery sack in my back pocket and, well. You know what happened next.

— How long did it take for her to stop breathing?

— 3 minutes.

— I honestly have no idea. Time just became sort of irrelevant. I was just in it. Nothing else was on my mind. I just know eventually I felt her kind of give up. She slumped. I felt her die.

ELIJAH: [offstage] A dead body revenges not injuries.

— I slid from the grasp of time's inexorable pull and felt only plastic and heat and pressure. I didn't know, but I knew. I heard him rustling beneath the kitchen sink and felt the possibility of violence secrete from his skin. I could smell it and I knew what was going to happen and I was not ready but ready.

— Do you regret it?

— No.

— Why not?

— I think if there was a way for me to get in contact with her now, she'd thank me.

— Let's ask it about the girl that got killed.

— Okay.

— What should we ask?

— Let's ask where she is.

— When I was 14, I remember my grandmother was basically comatose. Catatonic, whatever the word is. And she had this stay-at-home nurse. But he was gone for a few hours, and I was just there helping out. Turning her over so she didn't get bed sores. And I went over to fluff one of her pillows, and while I was holding it, it occurred to me that I could just put it over her face. I wouldn't even have had to hold down for very long, or very hard. She was so frail.

— "XXXXXXX, where are you right now?"

— "T"

— "H"

— "E"

— I honestly thought about doing it. Not because she looked miserable, not because it was the humane thing to do, but just because I wanted to. And right when I was about to do it, she opened her eyes. I think she knew. She died a few days later.

— Eric and Dylan made Doom levels that looked like their high school.

— No they didn't, they just made regular Doom levels you fucking idiot.

— It felt like high school to me.

— "E"

— "T"

— "E"

— "R"

— "N"

— "A"

— "L"

— Did you do it to anyone else?

— You can look at the court records. I'm already in jail for the rest of my fucking life. I don't need to think about it any more than I already have.

— Have you talked to her family at all?

— They came to visit once. I wasn't expecting them, and I wasn't sure what they'd say. It was just the mom and dad. The mom was the one with the phone, and the dad just stood next to her. He wouldn't look at me, but she did.

— What did she say?

— Nothing.

— We just looked at each other. I don't think she had anything she needed to say.

— Why did she come?

— I think she just wanted to see me.

— "H"

— "E"

— "L"

— "L"

— Did you know the girl was only 17?

— No.

— Would you have done it if you did know?

— I don't think it would have made a difference.

— I have been roused from death so many times I have stopped feeling dead. The dead suffer endlessly at the grief of the living.

— My buddy's uncle took over a TV news station once. He wanted to be broadcast, he had a message or something. But he had this stutter, and when they started filming, he couldn't get it out. He could only say like half a sentence. He would get stuck on a word and just say it over and over again before moving onto the next thought. He got so frustrated he cut off the interview about halfway through. Nobody got killed or anything. Except him I guess.

— I saw that live.

— That's the thing, they never aired it. It wasn't live. They just aired commercials while the police were outside, waiting to bust the door down.

— He had already killed himself by the time they got in.

— "R"

— "E"

— "V"

— "I"

— "V"

— "E"

— "S"

[Long silence]

— What the fuck does that mean?

— Do you remember how it happened, exactly?

— "YES"

— She was working at this factory hospital, just birthing babies one by one. The mothers were completely unconscious, and she would just pull them out in one *yoink*, clean them off and they'd move down the line. All day long, 8 hour shifts. At night she'd go home, and all she could think about were babies. She finally decided she'd had enough, and she threw one through a window. Then all the women on the line started doing it too. Infants flying through the air, soundless. The foreman couldn't stop them. They had to shut down the whole plant.

— I've been stuck here for, I don't even know how long.

— Ask her if she'll show us her tits.

— "NO"

— Come on, man, I'm sick of this game.

— When did she start sending you letters?

— I guess probably 2 years ago. The first one she kind of talked through her feelings. She really reamed me for doing what I did. For killing her daughter. There were some details I picked up on that seemed strange for her to tell me. Like, she casually mentioned she and her husband were having problems since it happened.

— Do you talk about that now?

— "YES"

— Yeah, it's funny, she says she didn't intend it that way.

— Years later, my best friend was dying. He had multiple sclerosis. When he started going downhill, it was so fast. It was like, I remember him having aches and sort of walking funny, and before I know it, he can't get out of bed, he's having trouble breathing. One day I was visiting him and he told me he didn't know if he could take much more of it. It all hurt so bad. And he asked me if I would do him a favor, a really important one. I said sure.

— You wouldn't believe how the dead are defiled. You wouldn't believe what the living do to us.

— He asked me if I'd kill him. He wanted it to be over but he didn't think he could do it himself. I don't know if he meant physically or emotionally. I never asked. But I said shit, that's a lot to ask of someone. He told me to think about it.

— I killed someone, too, you know. After I died.

— "YES"

— So, I did. A few visits passed, he didn't mention it. But one night I went over there and he asked about it again. And, you know, I had thought about it a lot, and I said I would. He asked if I'd do it right now. Nobody was with him, I was one of the few people who came by. He said, please. I thought really hard about it, and finally I decided that yeah, I would. I told him I was gonna smother him with a pillow, because that would look the least suspicious. No blood anyway. He said that would be fine. We watched a few episodes of something, I don't remember. One of the shows we always watched. Then he said, okay, I'm ready. I just held it down as tight as I could over his face, trying to plug holes where air could get through. He barely even struggled. I wasn't sad at the time. I was very sad after. But when I was doing it, all I could think about was my grandma.

ELIJAH: *[offstage]* The most sublime act is to set another before you.

— If I think about something hard enough, I can make it happen, or at least start to. And once I saw this kid walking around in one of those stupid kids t-shirts you can get at like Target or Wal-Mart, the ones that say stupid shit like "Who's the boss?" on them. And he was playing in his front yard and I saw someone walking around who I knew was up to no good and I shook the branches and did everything I could to direct their attention to the kid. And they saw him in the yard playing on a big plastic slide.

— What's your name, junior?

— And then they picked him up and took him away and everybody was talking about him like they were talking about me. And now he knows what it feels like. What you do to us.

— "GOOD BYE"

— The town was completely deserted, save for this one guy. He walked around to every house. He looked in every window, knocked on all the doors. Went in every shop. Looked in all the cars parked in the street. Checked under desks. Opened up manholes, went in the sewers. Called all the businesses in the phone book. Spent months looking for someone, anyone. All the electricity worked, the Internet worked, everything. Friends in other states would respond to his calls. But everyone in his town was gone. He didn't tell any of them, and none seemed to notice.

— What time is it?

— Hey, I've been looking for you. I got us drinks.

— Can we watch the one where Mac and Dennis buy a timeshare?

— "GOOD BYE"

— I guess I can do one more.

— Do you like monster trucks?

— "YES"

— I got a big remote controlled one that I don't know what to do with. Why don't you come out here and I give it to you?

— I know she's not awake, but do you think she's still hurting?

— "YES"

— We don't really know.

WILLIAM BLAKE: *[offstage]* I have also The Bible of Hell, which the world shall have whether they will or no.

— By the fourth or fifth letter, she had completely opened up. She opened one up by describing to me how conflicted she felt. She was having sex dreams about me. She described them in meticulous detail.

— We're having dinner at the restaurant **XXXXXXX** and I went to after the funeral and you ask me if I need to go to the bathroom and we go to the handicapped stall in the women's room and lock the door.

— It wasn't just her though.

— No, her husband had been sending them too.

— Same thing?

— He was more forthright about it from the getgo.

— My asshole opens up like a flowering rose even when I just think about your name.

— They must have been talking about it for a while. By this time, I had been in prison for maybe a decade. They started asking if we could meet again.

— Is it processing, do you think?

— "NO"

— I'm not sure what it is for them.

— You're so much better than me.

— I don't think we have much time left.

— Are the three of you happy?

— "YES"

— Please don't leave me here.

— I wish I could take it back but I can't.

— They're eating me alive.

— "NO"

— I miss having him around all the time. I watched him bend backwards and contort his shape and lose control of his body and shake and moan and I still fucking wish he was here even if it hurt him more because it hurts me more.

— I used to love you so much. But you can't stop picking at me, so now I hate you.

WILLIAM BLAKE: [offstage] The ancient tradition that the world will be consumed in fire at the end of six thousand years is true, as I have heard from Hell.

— Yeah. I think we are.

— "GOOD-BYE"

EVERY DA
REST OF Y

You see it on the sidewalk. It's a wad of fuzzy stuff and red stuff. It's dry and flat and smashed into the concrete. Your brain registers it as an animal, but cannot figure out which one. You're four years old.

"What is that?" you ask your mother, tugging at her hand.

She looks at it disapprovingly and tells you not to touch it.

It's a dead animal. They have diseases. You'll get sick.

That doesn't answer the question, but you know better than to argue, so you look at it one last time until your mom pulls you away by the arm and takes you into a Walgreens. She drags you around, buying things for her hair in bright plastic bottles, and you keep thinking about the flattened animal outside.

She lets go for a minute and you wander away, but not too far. She's looking at magazines as you wander to the aisle with dog treats and cat food. There are toys here, but you understand they're for animals so you don't get too excited.

But you do look. And when you see a big stick with a piece of string attached to a cartoony, fuzzy mouse, the image of the dead animal outside collides with this one. A dead mouse, smashed by something, eyes and little paws distended and broken, tied to a string tied to a stick.

You reach out. It's high up but you imagine the feeling of the fake fur on your fingers. You wonder what it will feel like, if it will feel old and dry like the thing outside. It's high up but you reach harder, standing on your tip-toes, your hand opening and closing in its direction.

"There you are," says your mother, grabbing you by the shoulder and pulling you away. "Those aren't for kids, they're for dogs and cats."

You look back and she tugs on your arm harder, forcing you to look in her eyes.

"That's exactly how John Walsh's son got kidnapped," she says to herself. Then to you: "Don't run away from me in the store."

These are your first memories.

⌒

You and your mom are at your mom's friend Gwen's house. Gwen and your mom are drinking wine and watching TV. You're in the living room with them, sitting against the wall playing with a kitten.

Gwen's cat Russell, who is a girl cat, ran away from home for a few days and came back with babies. Gwen was telling your mom about how she didn't know what to do with them, how she was going to try to put up flyers and see if anyone wanted to adopt the kittens. She was worried she was going to get stuck with eight cats and be a crazy cat lady.

This is the first time you've seen a cat up close. Most of the kittens are sleeping, but one starts crawling around on the floor and you pick it up with one hand and bring it over to the corner.

"Be careful!" says your mom sharply, but Gwen says it's okay, Russell picks them up with her mouth by the neck anyway. Your mom relaxes and they go back to watching TV.

You're sitting by the wall with the kitten and it's crawling all over you. It climbs up your arm and tries to get on your shoulder but you're both too small. Its claws hurt a little bit but you don't mind because it's the cutest thing you've ever seen and you want one of your own.

You throw a little ball with a bell inside and the kitten runs over to it and starts trying to bat it around with its paws. It's still too small to do much and you're not very good at physical activity yourself so you two are a perfect match. You pet its head hard and its head bobs up and down when your palm bops it between the ears.

The kitten bumps its head into your leg and mewls in the tiniest, highest pitch voice and you're overcome by emotion and you pick it up again and hug it.

You can hear it meowing in your arms and you think that must mean it likes it, so you hug it tighter and rock it back and forth, and its claws are digging into you, but they already were before, so you don't mind. You hug it and hug it and hug it because you love it, and you don't notice when it stops meowing until you feel it go limp in your arms and you know something isn't right. You let go hoping it will run off, but instead it falls to your lap and there's shit coming out of it and getting on your pants. You shake it with your hand and it still doesn't move.

You start screaming and then Gwen and your mom come over to see what happened and then they both start screaming, too.

Russell and the kittens make their way over to see what the commotion is about, and they start meowing and Russell taps at the dead kitten with her paw and whines, and it's the worst sound you've ever heard, and you cover your ears and scream as loud as you can. You say no no no no no no no over and over again and not only do you hate yourself for the first time, but you wish that you were dead instead of the kitten.

Your mom stops going over to Gwen's house.

The next morning it's the first thing you think of upon waking.

It will be the first thing you think of every morning for the rest of your life.

⌒

"You weird little queer."

It's after school and almost everyone has been picked up by their parents except you, because your mom works until 4:30 on

Tuesdays. You wait on the playground once they start locking up the school at 4:00. Most of the time you just read a book.

Today, Scott Tomlinson has his forearm pinning you across the chest to a chain link fence. You're looking into each other's eyes and he's breathing heavy. His breath smells like ass and it stings like onions. He has a big underbite and breathes out of his mouth. The teacher assigned to monitoring the playground is gone for the day. It's just you and Scott Tomlinson and his friend Daniel Stevens, who is standing behind Scott with his arms folded trying to look tough.

Scott Tomlinson doesn't like you, and you don't like him, but he's bigger than you. He tells everyone about how his grandpa signed him up for the Young Marines and how he learns survival skills and how the second he finishes school he's gonna join the real Marines and blow up Iraqis. You don't like him because his breath is bad and he doesn't like you because you're a skinny little fag.

He'd been eying you all week like he wants to murder you, and now is his chance. You don't think he's going to kill you but you understand that he probably could.

He asks you if you're scared and you aren't, you're just excited. You've been watching him look at you and you've been waiting for this. So you say no and he slams his arm into your chest and bounces you off the fence and asks how about now. And you feel like he's still not mad enough, so you spit in his face.

He pauses, but just for a second. Then, without pausing to wipe the wetness from his face, he rages and rockets his fists into your nose and cheekbones. Daniel Stevens starts kicking you in the stomach and back. There is blood pouring out of your nose and you can feel your ribs creak like a door hinge. Things are chipping and snapping and flaking away just below your skin, which can itself be so easily taken away.

It is the most amazing feeling in the world.

Scott Tomlinson and Daniel Stevens see blood on their shoes and hands and look down at you worried. You're crying and maybe even laughing a little. You're interrupted by a tide of vomit, and it pours out of your mouth and surrounds your head.

The teachers find you and you go to the hospital and you tell them what happened. Your mom presses charges against Scott Tomlinson and his dad pays your hospital bills. Daniel Stevens' parents send him to a reform school somewhere upstate.

The next time you see Scott is two weeks later, on your first day back at school. He has twin black eyes that have faded to purple rings. He looks like a raccoon. You laugh at him and he ignores you. Sometimes you catch him looking at you from across the lunchroom. You never say another word to each other.

This will be the second thing you think about every day for the rest of your life.

⌒

Click.

A cesarean section. The surgeon and his team move with blinding efficiency. The initial incision, at the base of the stomach, splits the first several layers of skin. A second finds purchase, revealing the opaque uterus. The surgeon carves deeper, into the placenta. Punctured, it bursts with a loud pop as the encased infant is bathed in light.

Click.

Low quality cell-phone footage, circa 2008. Grainy video shows what looks like a motorcycle accident. A man in leather stumbles around the site of the crash, holding his face. He turns, and the camera sees for the first time that his jaw is separated from his skull. Thick ribbons of flesh hang lazily from his cheekbones. He's trying to say something.

Click.

Montage of shotgun suicides set to blast beats and tinny, distorted guitars.

Click.

A drunken Ukranian falls from a concrete building, landing directly on his head. His body ragdolls, crumpling in a heap.

Click.

A man desperately clings to the top of an electrical tower. A storm has lit his body on fire. He can't decide whether to die falling or burning.

Click.

"We've already seen all of these."

"And?" you ask, scrolling. "Scoot over."

He types *animal crush video* into the search bar and hits enter. He scrolls and clicks and hits the "back" button and types some more. He knows you hate these and you don't need to tell him so. He's obsessed with watching them. You don't like them because you don't like watching anyone hurt anything, unless it's themselves. You know what it's like to get hurt and now all you think about, the thoughts that invade your head every morning right when you wake up, is what it would be like to go all the way. How it would feel to be completely pulverized. Ruined. Obliterated.

You scratch at the scabs on your thighs and feel some ooze a little. You want him to leave so you can make yourself feel better for a second.

He clicks on a video of a woman with big high heels on. There's a puppy on a pedestal. You think about the kitten and a few seconds later your friend is on the ground and your knuckles are split open. A delicate bead of blood pools at the corner of his mouth and he looks at you more confused than angry.

He gets up and runs out of your room and you don't stop him. You hear the front door slam and you're picking at your legs and hating yourself harder than ever. You catch your breath and hear a quiet squelching sound from your computer's speakers. You see what's on the screen and rip the power cable from the outlet and pull your hair and pace back and forth.

Your mom doesn't ask why he doesn't come over anymore. She was unnerved by his presence. In eight years, he will be arrested on murder charges after a bank robbery gone bad and she will tell you she always thought there was something screwy with that kid.

You'll scratch at your thighs and agree.

⌒

You get a job at a grocery store in the meat and seafood

department. Your job is to grind beef and cut steaks. You weigh meats for the customers. You fillet fish.

There is no college in your future and you don't like this job at all. You live in a studio in a decaying neighborhood. Your mom lives twenty miles away, in a trailer park. You don't get out to see her anymore, but you do talk every day. Whenever you do, she says that you could get a job you like better if you lived somewhere like where she lives. It would be less money. You wouldn't really have to work at all.

Sometimes, when your thoughts aren't racing, it sounds nice.

But you stick around at the grocery store for the way it smells. The aroma of cold tissue hangs thick in the air and you leave it on your skin long after you get home at night.

The customers are horrible. You don't eat meat yourself. When they ask for recommendations and you tell them so, they look at you and ask:

"What?"

"What is wrong with you?"

"Then why do you work in the fucking meat department?"

You say it's because they were hiring, and they wave their hands at you. Sometimes they try to get you written up. But you're an okay worker, and your manager just tells you to ignore them, that people are just rude sometimes. He's the other reason you stay here, because he doesn't give you any trouble.

Your coworkers don't love you but they don't hate you either. You don't have much to talk about with them anyway. You're the youngest person working here. All the nineteen-year-olds work as cashiers and stockers, but in the meat and seafood department it's you, a 40-year-old vet and a 60-year-old divorcee. The vet points out every woman wearing shorts or yoga pants and the divorcee complains about the vet doing this.

You listen to them argue, and when one of them says something you just nod without listening. They both think you're a space case, one of the only things they agree on. Sometimes they seem a little worried for you because you're so nervous all the time, but you don't care too much.

One day it's just you and the vet, and you're working the counter and he's at the back cubing up beef for stew chunks. You're wrapping up steaks and salmon and fresh bacon and he's talking to you about the war and you're kind of listening. There are a lot of customers because it's a Saturday, and you're trying to prevent a long line from forming. He just keeps slicing beef and talking about how, one night, Daesh suicide bombed their encampment, and you're not really sure if you believe him. He keeps talking and gets even more distracting and customers start yelling. That wet iron and tissue smell hangs thick in the air and you're sweating and wrapping meat and he's talking and talking until there's a horrible sound from the machine that forces you to turn around.

The vet looks at you and you look at the vet. His red face is now white, and he repeats, "my my my my my my my my my" and you look from his eyes to his shoulder down to his elbow to his wrist, and then there is nothing else to look at. Big waves of red pour out of what is left, a cross-section of hand that starts from the base of his thumb and cuts cleanly to his rightmost knuckle.

He turns and starts toward you and you can't take your eyes off it. You see the inside of his hand for just a moment and think about how it sort of looks like a rack of ribs.

He's asking you for help now and you're still paralyzed with fear. He's asking you for a towel and you're forgetting what that is. He sees your uselessness and walks from behind the counter in a daze, out into the aisle where horrified customers give him a wide berth. You walk to the back counter and look at the sink next to the meat slicer and you see his hand lying there bloodless and dead. You pick it up and wrap it in plastic wrap and put it in the freezer. It doesn't feel like his hand; it just feels like parts.

Someone is behind the counter with the stuttering vet trying to find a towel and asking you why you aren't helping. You don't really know.

The vet comes back to work a few weeks later. They have him as a cashier now. He still gets paid the same, and everybody feels sorry for him. You sometimes make eye contact when you're leaving for the night and he's counting down his register. You don't say anything and he doesn't either.

They keep you in the same department and for a few weeks

after it happened the store manager comes back behind the counter to make sure everything is okay. You're working the slicer now. They're worried about you.

Sometimes, when you're grinding beef or cubing it or slicing thin strips for stir frying, you worry too.

He's leaving because you're a fucking freak.

It's your birthday and you just worked a long shift. You took a brief call from your mother on your lunch break and she says happy birthday, did you get your card? She says her words with great care, savoring them. A little plastered.

There is going to be no card, and both of you know this. It will get lost in the mail. You're not worried. This is how things are now.

You text your boyfriend and he asks if he can come over later and you say sure, just give me a little while to get ready. I'll text you. I have a few things to do first.

You get home from your shift and you don't think twice about the big lump of blankets on your mattress. Your apartment is one room and a bathroom, and it's mostly bare. You take off your shirt and pick your laptop off the floor.

You've been researching meat processing. You've been downloading schematics. You've been learning about parts. You've been analyzing the process from beginning to end, from when the chickens and cows and pigs are huddled into narrow lines and hung upside down by their feet and bled out and skinned and crushed and filleted and ground and made into thick pastes and pates.

A few months ago, a former classmate you didn't know very well shared a video titled 'THE HORRORS OF FACTORY FARMING.' It was a series of quick cuts of animals being slaughtered all around the world. It instructed you to have compassion for the animals that are murdered for your sustenance.

You have something more than compassion.

You haven't watched any of those videos since that afternoon with your friend. You tried to forget the things you saw. But they force their way into your thoughts, just like the first two things you think about every morning when you wake up.

You can't stop thinking about it anyway. So you decide to learn.

You found one this morning that you couldn't finish before work. You press play and carry the laptop to the kitchen to get a glass of water. You half-watch. This time it's chickens, their necks broken, their bodies dunked in boiling water and their feathers plucked. Over and over again, down the line; alive, dead, alive, dead, alive, dead.

You think about the pressure of the neck-breaking device. You think about what it would be like, paralyzed but alive, to sink into the water and feel the flesh loosen from your bones, to feel the white hot intensity of the water as it blinds you.

You move to your floor mattress and lay down, video still playing. You feel a presence in the room with you. You were so engrossed you never felt it until it was right next to you. You throw off the blankets.

It's your boyfriend.

"Happy birthday!" he says.

You're startled and you throw your laptop aside and tell him he scared the shit out of you.

"What, did you have to jack off before I came over or something?"

He turns the laptop screen toward him. It's too late to stop him.

Thirty minutes later he's gone and you're alone again. You start to draft a text but you stop halfway through.

There's no point. He wouldn't get it.

⌒

Your mother is dead.

Her kidneys failed. She didn't tell you it was a problem. The last time you saw each other you could smell a little decay on her. It came out of her pores like pheromones. She was a quiet drunk. She'd have beer and Cheerios in the morning and put whiskey into decaf coffee in the evening. She complained of heartburn. You'd only talk on the phone for ten minutes at a time before the long silences would force one of you to hang up.

She's dead now, so there's no one to call anymore.

It's just you and a few of her friends at the funeral. Gwen is there. She comes over and half-heartedly offers her condolences. You say thank you and ask how she's been. She says fine and that she has to go.

You don't know what to do with her ashes, so you take them and toss handfuls into the river near her trailer. You'd never been to the park before. You were afraid to see what her life was like, but you were more afraid of her learning more about yours.

As you scoop the ashes from a plastic bag, the wind blows and carries her away in wisps, but it also brings the smell of something rotten and familiar. The smell of emulsifying tissue, of offal and fat melting against the heat of machinery, of animal shit and blood.

You scatter the rest of her ashes and follow your nose. The smell is overpowering, and you let it guide you away from the river and across the plains.

In the distance there is a building. You identify it as the source of the smell and you start to run toward it. As you get closer, you see a gravel parking lot and a fence. The smell burns your eyes until you're right up against it, and you can smell the rot and blood and plasma and the heat beating down on this enormous metal structure.

You understand this is what you've read so much about. This is where bodies are broken down, their most fundamental components destroyed and reincorporated until it's all the same paste. This is where the videos you now watch every night take place.

This is where animals, dying or dead, are pulverized.

This is where you want to spend the rest of your life.

∩

Tonight, the drive to paradise is made shorter by the absence of Highway Patrol. You turn onto the dirt road at the mile marker with the dog-eared corner. You hear the sound of crunching gravel beneath your tires. You flick the headlights off. Before long, the dark blur of a chain link fence bleeds into view, encasing the factory.

You've made this drive so many times, waiting for the perfect night. You could do it blindfolded.

This is how you've spent all your time since you found this place. You stopped going to work. You stopped charging your phone. You have a project that demands all your focus now. You're going to finish what started many years ago.

There's no one else in the parking lot. You know this by now. You've never parked in it, opting to ditch your car miles away when you made excursions inside, long after the plant closed. With no flashlight to guide you, you place your hand on the outer wall and glide it across the exterior to find your way in.

You pick the padlock on a side door. You've been practicing.

The door squeaks open.

Inside it's pitch black. There's no need for lights. You know what it's like in here by now. You can get around through instinct. Fourteen big steps from the door, straight forward. One half-step to the right and you're in front of it.

A complex maze of machinery. Hundreds of parts. Multiple ladders and steps. When you first started coming here, you assumed the equipment would be clean from the end of the day, but this isn't like in the manufacturer's videos. The smell is overwhelming, the putrid stench lighting up your nose and still, after all this time, forcing you to stifle bile.

Standing, waiting. Then, a deep breath.

You're running your hands all along the edges, feeling the corners, pressing down on screws and sharp corners with your palms until it hurts. The cold alloy warms at your touch, soaking up your heat.

Tonight, you decide, will be the night.

You strip off your shirt and unbutton your pants. You scurry out of socks and underwear. You fold each item and place it in a pile, making note of where you left it by the first set of steps.

You stand at the base, admiring the dim outlines of components. Flip a few switches and this whole thing would roar to life. You know where they all are, but you aren't ready.

Not yet.

You fumble toward the ladder, next to the elevator shaft. Hand over hand, all the way to the top, the smell growing stronger and stronger until at last, you reach the summit. This is the hard part, the one you haven't tested yet: a drop, one which requires throwing both feet over the side of the elevator car and plunging directly into the container below. You savor the moment.

Then, you push off, hard. The second it takes to hit the bottom feels like a lifetime, but the impact is broken by the cold, wet pile at your feet. The pain radiates from your heels up your shins to your knees. You remember Scott Tomlinson and you remember your friend in your room. The smell almost knocks you out, but you regain composure.

Examining your surroundings, now totally blinded by darkness, you feel the contents of the material buffer bin. Hooves. What feels like a paw. Feathers. Unidentifiable carcasses, crudely shredded in halves and quarters. Limbs. Grease. Organs.

You're sucking in lungfuls of the reeking carrion aroma. You planned to delay your gratification, but this is your one
shot.

On your knees now, scraping the edges, scooping up as much liquid as possible with both hands, sacramentally. Rubbing it into your arms, legs, hair. Avoiding the retracted blades to your best ability but sometimes grazing your arm against them anyway, feeling little cuts open all over. Reaching down into the pipe that carries the five centimeter chunks down to the pre-crusher. Feeling what you know to be the grey remnants of untold amounts of meat; for pet food, for prisoner rations.

Praying to be rendered.

You lay in it, on your back, covering yourself with the fibrous slop like a blanket. You stay here for a long time, not thinking, barely breathing, until you start to feel the meat come alive. Just like you knew it would.

What you wouldn't give for the switches to flip themselves. Soon, you will make a choice. You will climb down from here, covered in it, and make the machine come to life. You will decide whether to become one with yourself or to walk away. You will decide very soon. But for now, you lay here, in the slop, arms resting against the edges of great blades that may soon put an end to you.

Your mind is clear as you pull the guts over your head.

You know what choice to make.

ACKNOWLEDGEMENTS

I am forever indebted to Elle Nash, Jane DIESEL, Anthony Dragonetti, B.R. Yeager, Henry Goodridge, John Samuel Brown, Clara Creavin and Jordan Perkic for their editorial assistance and valuable insight throughout the compilation of this manuscript.

My sincerest thanks to all the editors at the various publications that ran early versions of these stories for giving me a shot.

Thank you to Christopher Norris and Mike Corrao for giving this new edition a whole new look and feel, and for getting what I'm going for.

Extreme gratitude to Benjamin DeVos for adopting my book and treating it with so much care.

Thank you to my mother and father, Megan and Robert Jacobson, and my siblings, Gabriella, Rylan and Liam, for being the most supportive family a girl could ask for.

Most of all, thank you to Megan Robinson, for gassing me up more than anyone. I miss you every single day.